GUARDED DESIRES

ANNA STONE

Cover by Kasmit Covers

ISBN: 9781922685001

CHAPTER 1

Carmen scanned the ballroom from her vantage point at the back of the room, keeping a lookout for any signs of trouble. The charity auction was about to start, and the guests were trickling in. Dressed in tuxedos and evening gowns, diamonds and pearls, they were the city's elite, the richest and most influential.

But Carmen's job tonight wasn't to protect these people, or even the millions of dollars of valuables to be auctioned off at the event. She was part of a different elite, part of a team of professional bodyguards tasked with protecting a single woman—Amber Pryce.

The Pryces were one of the wealthiest, most powerful families in the country, and Amber was the sole Pryce heir. The night's auction was just one of the many charitable events she ran for her company. But despite her wealth, she wasn't another spoiled socialite. She was a powerhouse of a woman, one whose domineering nature had earned her a formidable reputation.

But Carmen hadn't met her yet. Everything she knew of Amber Pryce came from rumors and gossip.

She focused her attention on the room before her. She couldn't afford to let her guard down. Tonight's job was about more than just the auction. It was a trial run, an audition of sorts, for a more permanent contract as part of Amber's personal bodyguard team. Amber had fired her old security team, apparently out of dissatisfaction. That told Carmen all she needed to know about her client's expectations.

As she stood by, one of her colleagues approached. Hudson. The dark-haired man was almost 30, a few years older than her. Not that he acted like it.

He gave her a nod before taking his place beside her. "Hey, Torres."

"Hudson," she replied.

He adjusted the jacket of his tuxedo. "Whose idea was it to put us in these stupid suits? It's like wearing a straitjacket."

"Stop fidgeting," she said. "You're going to draw attention."

Amber wanted a full security detail, but she wanted everyone to blend in, so the entire team was dressed in suits, just like the servers and staff. It all seemed like overkill. Was it just the paranoia of another rich client, or something else?

But it wasn't Carmen's job to question orders. It was her job to protect her client. And she took that job seriously.

Hudson gave her a nudge and nodded toward an older woman dressed in a gaudy, diamond-encrusted gown.

"You'd look good in one of those dresses. Some high heels too."

"Probably." When she wasn't on a job, Carmen wore dresses as easily as she wore suits. "And even in a dress and heels, I could still kick your ass."

Hudson smirked. "Is that humor? Looks like someone's finally starting to loosen up."

"I wasn't joking." She'd joined the team years ago, and everyone she worked with still gave her a hard time about her serious attitude.

But it was nothing more than friendly ribbing, the kind that was a sign she'd been accepted as one of them. It had taken her some time to infiltrate the boys' club that the team was, but once she'd proved she could hold her own, she'd been quickly accepted.

And hold her own she could. She was strong for her size, and what she lacked in strength she made up for in physical and mental agility. She could take down a man twice her size before he even knew what was happening.

Demonstrating this on a skeptical Hudson in front of all their colleagues was exactly how she'd proved that she was as capable as the rest of them, if not more.

After all, she was a Marine. She'd served four years, enlisting right out of high school. She'd planned to reenlist after her initial term, but after the death of her grandmother, she'd left to take over as her sister's guardian.

It had been a difficult decision to make. But her sister had needed her. Their parents had been killed when they were young, and she had no one else. So the past few years of Carmen's life had been spent raising her teenage sister, sacrificing not only her career in the Marines, but her personal life.

However, it was a small sacrifice to make. And soon after leaving the Marines, she'd been recruited to join the elite bodyguard team she was part of. Her job gave her a similar sense of purpose as the Marines had.

Their boss approached them. Wheeler was older, and an Army veteran, but the only sign of his age was the specks of gray in his black hair.

"Hudson, I need you at the entrance," he said. "I want more eyes on the new arrivals."

Hudson nodded. "Yes, boss."

As he marched off, Wheeler turned to Carmen. "I want you on Pryce, personally. Don't let her out of your sight, but keep your distance. These old-money types, they don't want an entourage following them around like they're celebrities. They want us grunts to be invisible. So don't get too close. Pryce is one woman you do *not* want to piss off."

Carmen nodded. "Got it."

Wheeler wasn't big on formality, despite the fact that most of the team had a military background. It had taken Carmen a long time to get out of the habit of speaking to him like a superior officer. She'd had trouble adjusting to civilian life, initially. She'd always liked the structure and discipline of the Marines.

"Speak of the devil," he said.

She turned, following his line of sight. Striding toward them was a woman, the crowd parting before her as she passed through it. She was tall, with a crown of golden blonde hair pinned up on her head. Her dark blue evening gown was embroidered with silver, and her diamond necklace and glittering heels sparkled in the chandelier light.

Amber Pryce. Carmen had seen her before, in magazines, on the news. But in person, she was breathtaking. Every part of her was flawless, from her glacial blue eyes to her sculpted cheekbones, her hourglass figure carved out of ice. She had this boldness about her, this undeniable confidence that dominated the room.

The women of the Pryce family had a reputation for their fierceness. Rumor had it that several generations ago, the wife of the Pryce patriarch had murdered her abusive husband before making off with all his wealth. On her deathbed, she'd made her daughter pledge to never let a man get his hands on the family money, beginning the tradition of a long line of Pryce matriarchs ruling the family.

It was just a rumor. But it fit the image that the Pryce women held, and Amber was no exception. She was a picture of feminine strength and beauty.

A queen.

Amber stopped before them. "Wheeler, was it?" Her tone was polite but firm.

"Yes, ma'am," he replied. "What can I do for you?"

"Send someone to check the courtyard," she ordered. "We can't have anyone unsavory sneaking in. And the auction is about to start, so be on your guard."

Wheeler nodded. "Yes, ma'am."

Carmen had never seen her boss behave so deferentially. And what did Amber mean by 'unsavory'? Was there a more serious threat at play here than Carmen knew?

Suddenly, Amber turned to her, her eyes meeting

Carmen's for the first time.

A shiver went through her. There was something in Amber's gaze, something cool and commanding, that made her heart race. Those eyes, piercing and blue, seemed to want something from her. Those lips, ruby red, seemed to whisper something to her. Her unwavering expression, it demanded something of her...

Carmen drew in a breath, trying to settle her pulse. Why was Amber making her feel this way? She wasn't the kind of woman to be intimidated by anyone.

But intimidated wasn't what she was feeling.

"Torres?" Wheeler interjected. "You all right?"

Carmen snapped out of her trance, nodding. "I'm fine."

She glanced at her boss, then back at Amber. But now, the cool fire in the woman's eyes was gone, replaced by her earlier haughtiness.

"I'll send some men to watch the courtyard," Wheeler said. "And Torres here is going to be keeping an eye on you personally tonight. She's one of our best."

Amber looked Carmen up and down. "Torres. Do you have a first name?"

"It's Carmen," she said.

"Keep your eyes open, Carmen. I can't afford to have any trouble tonight."

Carmen nodded, her mouth suddenly too dry to form words. What was wrong with her? She should have been more annoyed about Amber's presumptuousness than she was. *Keep your eyes open?* She knew how to do her job. She was a professional.

So why was she acting like a bumbling idiot who could barely speak?

Amber huffed. "I need to go prepare for the auction."

With that, she turned and walked away, parting the crowd before her once more.

Carmen's boss barked in her ear. "What are you gaping at her for? Follow her."

Carmen shook her head. "Yes. Right away."

He frowned. "I told that woman you're one of the best because it's true. Don't let me down."

"I won't."

With a nod to Wheeler, she followed in Amber's wake.

Carmen stood in the wings, just out of view, watching the crowd as Amber spoke on stage. The auction was wrapping up, and according to Amber's speech, it had been a rousing success.

"I'd like to thank everyone who contributed tonight," Amber said. "Your generous contributions will go a long way toward funding programs for the youth of our city."

The audience watched her, captivated. While Carmen had no interest in Amber's talk of foundations and funding, there was something mesmerizing about the way Amber spoke. She commanded the crowd, held them in sway with her velvet-smooth voice, seduced them with her hypnotic gaze...

Carmen pried her eyes away from her, focusing instead on their surroundings. She had a job to do. But the night had been uneventful in that regard. She'd spent the last few hours trailing Amber while she shook hands and made small talk. It was dull, but no duller than Carmen's usual jobs. And she'd spent plenty of time in the Marines doing nothing.

"And finally," Amber said. "I'd like to thank those who worked so hard tonight to make this event possible. The catering staff, the decorators, security…"

Carmen suppressed a scoff. *How nice of her to thank us servants.*

Amber finished off her speech to rousing applause. She left the stage, where she was immediately accosted by a local politician, who she greeted with a smile and a firm handshake. Carmen had to hand it to the woman. She knew how to work a room. No, how to own it.

Soon, a photographer appeared beside Amber, taking her aside and gesturing toward the doors to the ballroom. From what Carmen could make out, Amber was needed outside for photos.

Amber gave the man a nod before following him toward the doors. Carmen edged her way through the crowd in their wake, taking care to stay an appropriate distance away while still keeping her client in sight.

As Amber reached the doors, she glanced backward at Carmen, just for a moment. Was it simply to confirm that Carmen was still there guarding her? More than once, she had caught Amber looking at her with an intensity that sent heat rising through her…

Carmen shook her head. Other than their brief exchange at the start of the event, Amber hadn't spoken a single word to her. Considering how she seemed to render Carmen unable to speak, that was probably a good thing.

Outside, on the circular driveway leading up to the hall, a group of guests were gathered before a huddle of photographers from different media outlets. Carmen recognized a few of the guests as the women Amber owned her company with, along with other prominent local figures.

As Amber joined them, Carmen exchanged a brief nod with Wheeler and Hudson by the entrance before returning her attention to Amber, who was being directed to pose with the others. Everyone at the event, from the guests to the staff, had been thoroughly vetted. They were unlikely to pose any threat to Amber. However, out here in the open, she was much more exposed. Carmen needed to stay alert.

Finally, the photographers dismissed the group. The crowd dispersed, most of the guests remaining outside to converse in the cool night air.

As Carmen stood by, waiting for Amber, the sound of a car engine reached her ears. She turned toward it, peering down the dimly lit driveway. A car was approaching, but it didn't have its headlights on.

She took a few steps toward where Amber stood, just a couple of feet from the edge of the driveway. She hadn't reacted to the car. Neither had anyone else.

But something wasn't right. There shouldn't have been any cars on the driveway at all right now. And the car wasn't slowing down. It was picking up speed.

The hairs on the back of Carmen's neck stood up. At the same time, Amber turned toward the car, finally noticing it. If it continued to follow the path of the circular driveway, it would drive right past them.

But it was coming at them too fast, too erratically.

And Amber was right in its path.

The car's engine roared. A surge of adrenaline shot through Carmen's veins. She had less than a second to act.

She moved on instinct, crashing against Amber as she tackled her to the ground. Behind her, the car's wheels screeched, drowning out the gasps of the onlooking crowd. Shielding Amber with her body, Carmen turned her head toward the car. It swerved back onto the driveway, continuing down it until it disappeared into the night.

She let out a breath. Pulse thundering in her ears, she looked down at Amber. The woman's face had gone pale. And for the first time that night, she saw Amber's composure slip away, only to be replaced by something else.

Fear.

Suddenly, Carmen was blinded by a series of flashes. Cameras. She blinked, her surroundings coalescing around her. Here she was, practically lying on top of Amber Pryce, looking down into her eyes in front of a watching crowd.

She scrambled off her client and crouched down beside her. "Are you all right?"

Amber nodded and sat up, brushing herself off. As she did, Carmen noticed a long, jagged tear in the skirt of her evening gown. Carmen winced. The dress looked like it cost more than her entire salary.

Amber gave her a sharp look. "A hand, if you will?"

"Sure." Carmen held out her hand. Amber took it, a spark of electricity arcing between them.

She pulled Amber to her feet carefully, holding her free hand out to support her in case she was unsteady. But Amber wasn't unsteady. Her usual composure had returned. It was as if nothing had happened at all.

Had Carmen imagined the fear in her eyes just moments ago? Now, she was looking at Carmen with that same piercing gaze as before. And Carmen still had a hold of her hand. When she'd pulled Amber to her feet, they'd ended up standing close, barely a foot from each other, and Carmen could feel her heat, could breathe her scent, a cool, sweet fragrance with an intoxicating tinge of spice—

"Ms. Pryce!"

That was Wheeler's voice. Carmen turned to see him rushing toward them. She dropped Amber's hand, stepping back to a more respectable distance.

Wheeler swooped in to check that Amber was unharmed, offering repeated apologies. He turned to Hudson nearby. "Did you get the license plate?"

Hudson shook his head. "It was too dark. It was probably just a guest who had too many drinks."

Carmen retreated to the side quietly. The adrenaline had dissipated, but she still felt something smoldering inside, that fire that had sparked when her hand had touched Amber's.

Or maybe it was just embarrassment. After all, she'd tackled her client and torn her gown in front of two dozen people. Maybe she'd been a little overzealous.

Hudson appeared beside her, his expression confirming her doubts. "What was that?" he said. "That car wasn't anywhere near her."

Was he right? Had it just been a drunk guest? Someone distracted, who had forgotten to turn on their headlights? Perhaps the car hadn't been coming for Amber after all.

She glanced toward Amber. Her heart skipped a beat. The woman was looking back at her, arms crossed. Carmen couldn't read her expression, but she didn't need to.

Amber Pryce was *not* happy.

Had Carmen just screwed up the job for the entire team?

CHAPTER 2

Amber entered the Mistress Media offices. It was early in the morning, so the sprawling sea of glass and desks on the top floor of the high-rise building was empty. However, within a few hours, it would be teeming with people.

She made her way to her office and took a seat in the leather chair behind her desk, taking a moment to survey her realm through the glass walls. She was one of five owners of Mistress Media, a female-led multimedia company that had been started by a close friend of hers more than five years ago. Since then, it had grown into a multi-billion-dollar empire.

Amber's role at Mistress was to head the company's nonprofit wing. She took her work seriously, even though she didn't need a job in the conventional sense. Her family had made their fortune generations ago, and she was set to inherit it all.

But that didn't mean Amber was expected to do nothing other than live a life of leisure. The reality was far from it.

As her mother liked to remind her, her job was to simply be a Pryce, to represent the family and its interests.

And one day, perhaps sooner rather than later, she was expected to take over her mother's role as the head of the Pryce family. On the surface, that meant sitting on the board of their family company and running their family's charity foundation. But beyond that, she was expected to become the public face of the Pryces, to use the power, wealth, and influence that came with the family name to further their interests.

She'd been raised for this life from birth, raised with the expectation that she'd become someone influential. She had been groomed for leadership, molded into the perfect example of feminine charm, strength, and power, all so that she could one day take up her mother's throne.

And while she had every intention of doing that, she also wanted the freedom to live a life of her choosing. So when her friend Madison Sloane had come to her years ago with the idea for Mistress Media, which included a considerable nonprofit wing run by Amber, she'd jumped at the opportunity.

She settled in her seat and opened her laptop, checking her schedule for the day. She barely had a spare moment. And she'd left herself a note to call her mother, who was recuperating from surgery. Amber had been getting regular updates from her nurse, but she hadn't spoken to her mother personally in days.

The two of them had a fraught relationship. Her mother had always disapproved of her life choices. She hated that Amber had chosen to use her talents outside of the family, here at Mistress. She felt that Amber needed to focus on her legacy, on the family she would one day be the head of.

But her mother's disapproval went beyond Amber's job. While Pryce women had always been unconventional, rejecting traditional gender roles and prizing independence, her mother still believed in the importance of family. And the fact that Amber wasn't interested in a husband and children was a major source of her mother's displeasure. Amber was 34 now, which her mother felt was far too old to not have settled down.

But Amber had no interest in any of that. While she didn't begrudge the idea of settling down eventually, she wasn't in a hurry. And she had no intention of settling down with a man.

A woman, on the other hand…

But what she sought in a woman was hard to find. Amber wanted someone who was her equal, who wouldn't be intimidated by her money and status. She wanted someone confident and decisive, strong enough to hold her own.

But at the same time, she required someone who would defer to her in other areas, namely inside the bedroom.

Did such a contradiction of a woman even exist?

There was a knock on her door. She looked up to find Madison, the company's CEO, strolling into the room.

"Good morning." She took a seat in front of Amber's desk. "You're here early."

"Just getting a head start on all this work," Amber replied. "After last night, I have a busy day ahead of me."

"I can imagine. Do you know how much we raised?"

"I don't have the final numbers yet, but it's in the ballpark of five million. We broke last year's record."

"Wonderful. Congratulations on another successful event."

"It was nothing. Getting the wealthy to part with their money so they can feel good about being charitable is hardly a challenge."

Amber had been practically bred for the job. Her upbringing and name meant she had connections in high places and could navigate high society with ease. With her natural charisma and persuasiveness, whatever she set her mind on was hers for the taking.

"I heard there was an incident outside the event last night," Madison said. "After we took photos."

"Ah, yes." Amber waved a dismissive hand. "It was a minor misunderstanding, that's all."

Madison studied her face. "Are you all right?"

"Other than a bruise or two, I'm none the worse for wear. I can't say the same for my gown." It was such a beautiful dress, and bespoke at that, but Amber could always have the designer make her another one.

"I'm glad you're all right. I'll leave you to it, then." Madison rose from her chair. "Oh, and Blair wants to speak to you about an article she's writing. Something about influential women. She wants to do a profile on you." Blair was Madison's wife and a journalist for Mistress Media.

"Tell her to come by this afternoon. I'll be in the office until evening, but I have a dinner meeting with Councilwoman Reid tonight." It was all in a day's work for a Pryce.

As Madison left the room, Amber's mind returned to the incident outside the auction. Whoever had been driving that car hadn't really been trying to run her over, had they? Had it just been a false alarm?

But she couldn't shake the sense of dread she'd felt the moment she'd spotted the car barreling toward her. What if it hadn't been an accident after all?

What if the person who had been behind the wheel of the car was the very person who'd been stalking her for the past few months?

But Amber had very little evidence that anyone was stalking her. There were the letters, but they could simply have been from an overzealous fan. Her wealth and status tended to attract the occasional admirer.

However, the letters were becoming increasingly erratic and threatening, increasingly personal. Whoever was writing them knew a little too much about her. Had they gotten close to her, somehow, without her knowing it? Was that why she had the constant feeling she was being watched?

It was just a feeling. But her instincts had never been wrong. She trusted them. And they were telling her to be alert, just like they'd told her last night.

And that wasn't all her instincts had told her the night of the auction. They'd told her that she'd finally found a replacement for her old security detail. She'd fired her old team because they hadn't taken her concerns seriously. But the bodyguard team from last night had demonstrated they were serious about her safety, one bodyguard in particular.

Carmen Torres. Amber didn't pay much mind to the people who worked for her, but Carmen had captured her attention the moment she'd laid eyes on her. She had a strong yet understated beauty that Amber found striking.

Golden bronze skin, a fit build, curves that the suit she'd worn had been unable to hide. Deep brown eyes, ringed with the kind of long, thick lashes some women went to great lengths to imitate. While her hair had been pulled back into a practical ponytail, the dark, luscious waves had seemed like they were trying to break free.

But that wasn't what had drawn Amber's attention. Carmen had this silent intensity about her, her soft, feminine features at odds with the hard look in her eyes.

And when Amber looked at her, her eyes had revealed something else, the faintest flicker of lust like a candle in the darkness.

A smile pulled at Amber's lips. She liked women like Carmen. She liked the challenge of stripping away their tough veneer to get to what lay beneath.

If she was to strip Carmen bare, what would she find?

She pushed the thought aside. None of that mattered. What mattered was that Carmen had reacted to a potential threat when no one else had. *She* hadn't thought it was a false alarm. And neither did Amber.

Carmen was exactly who she needed.

She took her phone and dialed the number for Henry Wheeler.

He answered the call promptly. "Ms. Pryce. What can I do for you?"

"I need to see Carmen Torres," she said.

CHAPTER 3

Carmen wandered into the kitchen in search of coffee. She'd slept in after the long night she'd had. She wanted nothing more than to curl back up in bed, but she was more disciplined than that.

As she entered the kitchen, she found a pot of coffee already brewed. Was her sister home? And since when did she drink coffee? She'd always hated the taste as a kid. While Jo was 18 now, Carmen found it hard to think of her sister as anything other than a gangly girl.

She poured herself a cup of coffee before finding her sister in the living room, perched on the couch with her laptop on her lap.

"Morning," Carmen said. "Why aren't you at school yet?"

"No school today," Jo replied. "It's a teacher admin day. I told you about it last week."

"Right. I must have forgotten."

Jo raised an eyebrow. "Looks like someone had a big night."

"You could say that." After unceremoniously tackling her

19

client and damaging her expensive dress, Carmen had spent the rest of the night avoiding both Amber and her boss. Wheeler clearly wasn't happy with her, especially since the job had been a trial for a more permanent contract. She doubted that Amber would want to hire the team now.

"You didn't tell me your job last night was for Amber Pryce," Jo said.

Carmen frowned. "How do you know that?"

"You haven't seen the photos?"

"What photos?"

Grinning, Jo turned her laptop screen toward Carmen. "You're famous."

On the screen was a series of photos, all taken at the charity auction, outside. They showed Carmen on top of Amber, moments after knocking her to the ground, along with a few shots of Carmen helping her up afterward, their hands clasped together.

Carmen groaned. Somehow, the photos looked far more suggestive than the reality. If her boss wasn't furious with her already, he would be after seeing these photos. Amber had stressed how much she wanted her bodyguards to remain invisible and Carmen had created a scene in front of half a dozen photographers.

"So, what happened?" Jo asked.

"Nothing," Carmen replied. "I was just doing my job."

She was a professional, after all. What happened last night had just been a part of that.

So why did Carmen keep going over the events of the evening in her head? Why couldn't she get Amber out of her mind? She wasn't the type to be starstruck by someone like Amber Pryce. And she'd worked with famous clients before.

No, it wasn't Amber's fame that had Carmen all worked up. It was Amber herself. There was something about her that got under Carmen's skin, and she was uncertain whether it was in a good way or a bad way. Amber was alluring and bold, domineering and demanding. And although the two of them had barely spoken a word to each other, every time their eyes met, Carmen had felt something stir inside her.

"Whatever you say." Jo closed her laptop and put it aside. "By the way, I wanted to talk to you about college."

Carmen snapped back to reality. She knew this moment was coming. Her sister was an adult now. It was only natural that she'd want to start living her life and becoming independent.

But was Jo really ready for that? Was Carmen? She'd been raising Jo all by herself for years now. Their parents had been killed when Carmen was a child, and Jo barely more than a toddler. Their abuela had taken them in, raising them both, until a car accident had stolen her from them. They'd been left with no other family, at least not here in the States.

So Carmen had stepped in as Jo's guardian, sacrificing her career in the Marines. But in a way, Jo was the reason she'd joined the Marines in the first place. After their parents' deaths, after she'd failed to protect her family that night, Carmen had vowed to become someone strong enough to protect those she loved, along with anyone else who needed it.

Jo had needed her. So Carmen had done her best to look after her, to keep her safe and happy.

But she couldn't protect her forever.

"All right," she said. "What do you—"

Carmen's phone began to ring. It was her boss. She stifled a curse. She didn't have work today, but she could guess why he was calling.

"Hold that thought," she said.

She went into the kitchen and answered the call.

Wheeler's gruff voice came over the phone. "Morning, Torres. Amber Pryce called. She wants to see you."

Carmen frowned. "Pryce wants to see me? Why?"

"She didn't say. Your guess is as good as mine."

The only thing Carmen could think of was that Amber wanted to tell her off personally for tackling her and ruining her designer gown.

"She insisted on it," Wheeler said. "She's refusing to discuss the contract any further until she's spoken to you personally."

Carmen sighed. She wasn't getting out of this. "Okay. When does she want to see me?"

"Six p.m. today, at her office. This contract is riding on it, so do *not* mess this up."

Carmen hung up the phone. After what had happened the night before, she'd never expected to see Amber again. And given the way she seemed to lose her wits around Amber, she wasn't sure she wanted to.

But what did Amber want from her?

She returned to the living room. "Sorry, that was work. What were you saying about college?"

Jo shook her head. "It doesn't matter. Amber Pryce wants to see you? Why?"

"Stop eavesdropping. And yes, she does. For professional reasons, obviously."

Her sister gave her a cheeky smile. "I don't know, those photos from last night don't look professional at all."

Carmen ignored her. Amber was nothing more than another client. No, a *potential* client. And Carmen had to salvage things with her for the sake of the team.

Amber stood by the floor-to-ceiling windows of her office, awaiting the bodyguard's arrival. It was almost six p.m., and she had a short window of time to meet with Carmen before her dinner meeting.

She walked over to the drinks cabinet in the corner and withdrew a bottle of scotch and a glass. As she began to pour, someone cleared their throat behind her.

She turned. Carmen stood in the doorway, dressed in jeans and a leather jacket, her dark, shoulder-length hair loose. While her appearance was more casual than the night before, she still held herself with that same on-guard manner.

"Miss Torres." Amber looked at her watch. "Six p.m., and not a moment later."

Was that Carmen's military background coming into play? Amber had carried out a rudimentary background check on Carmen earlier. What she'd discovered both impressed and puzzled her.

"Come in," she said. "And shut the door."

Carmen stepped into the office and closed the door behind her.

Amber gestured for her to take a seat in a nearby chair. Carmen sat down stiffly. Did the woman ever drop her guard? That wasn't a bad thing. After all, that was why Amber had called her here.

But at the same time, it made Amber even more intrigued by her. What was behind the woman's stone facade? What would it feel like to chip it away, piece by piece?

Amber remembered herself. "Would you like something to drink?" She gestured toward the well-stocked drinks cabinet.

Carmen shook her head. Amber finished pouring her scotch, then took a seat in the armchair across from Carmen. She swirled her drink around before bringing it to her lips, savoring the aroma and taste. All the while, Carmen watched her silently, her dark eyes giving no sign as to what lay behind them.

Amber set her drink down and folded her hands in her lap. "Miss Torres. May I call you Carmen?"

Carmen nodded. "Whatever you like, ma'am."

"There it is again, that military discipline. You may call me Amber. Or Ms. Pryce, if you insist on being formal."

Carmen hesitated. "All right. Amber."

"No need to be so tense. I simply wanted to speak to you about last night."

Carmen winced. "Sorry about that."

"Sorry? Why would you be sorry?"

"Because I tackled you and ruined your dress."

"You think I'm angry about that? I can always buy another." Amber studied Carmen's face. "Is that why you think I called you here? To dress you down for ripping my evening gown?"

"Well, yes." Carmen paused. "If that's not why you called me here, why did you want to see me?"

Amber picked up her glass and took a long, slow sip of her scotch before setting it down again. "I called you here because I want you to be my personal bodyguard."

Carmen frowned. "What? Why?"

"Isn't it obvious?" Amber leaned forward, her gaze locked on Carmen's. "You got my attention last night. In a good way."

Something flickered in Carmen's eyes. Surprise. Hesitation. And something else, something almost like desire.

Amber held back a smile. So this tough, stoic bodyguard wasn't unflappable.

"I don't understand," Carmen said.

"It's simple. You were tasked with protecting me last night. You saw a potential threat, and you took appropriate action. I saw that car. I sensed, in that moment, that it was coming for me. And whether or not that threat was real, you reacted to it. That's more than I can say for anyone else on your team, or my previous bodyguard teams."

"Teams? What happened to them?"

"I fired them for not taking my safety concerns seriously," Amber said.

"And what are those concerns, exactly?"

"Well, there are the usual concerns that come with being the sole heiress to a family fortune worth billions. But beyond that, I have reason to believe there's a stalker on my tail." Amber sat back and crossed her legs. "I'll tell you more after you accept the job. You and the rest of your team, of course. I'll need a full security detail, but I want you with me personally at all times. I've already discussed the details of the contract with Wheeler. Your team will be paid at 50 percent above your usual rate, and as my personal bodyguard, you'll receive a bonus on top of that. It's a three-month contract initially, after which I'll consider a more long-term arrangement."

"And if I say no? Will you still give the team the contract?"

"Are you saying no?" Amber asked. "If you have any issues with what I've proposed, by all means, speak up."

Carmen was silent for a moment. "How did you know I'm military?

"I did a background check on you. And given your background, I'm confident you're up for the job. You were in the Marines for four years. You were rising up the ranks, had a promising career ahead of you. But then, you chose not to reenlist."

"I had my reasons."

"I'm sure you did. Regardless, you have an impressive background, and you've proved to be competent. You're exactly who I need by my side." Amber folded her arms across her chest. "I need an answer from you, Carmen. I chose you for this job because of your decisiveness. And I don't make mistakes."

Nevertheless, Carmen didn't respond immediately. A second passed, then another. But she was simply delaying the inevitable. She wanted to say yes. Amber could see it in her eyes.

So why the hesitation?

Finally, Carmen spoke. "All right. I'll take the job. But if we're going to do this, I'll need to know exactly what's going on with this stalker."

"Certainly," Amber said. "And I'll tell you everything when you start work tomorrow. I want you and your team at the Pryce residence at eight a.m., understood?"

Carmen gave her a curt nod. "Understood. Is there anything else?"

"No, that's all." Amber rose from her chair. "If you'll excuse me, I have a dinner engagement to get to."

She watched Carmen leave the room, following her through the glass walls of the office with her gaze. But even after she disappeared from view, an image of her remained in Amber's mind, clear as crystal.

Amber liked the woman. It was obvious that she took her job seriously, conducted herself like a consummate professional. Amber respected that. She too had been trained to conduct herself in a way that projected an image of unwavering self-assuredness, to never let any emotions or desires show, to never give in to them, except in private.

Was that why she found Carmen so enticing? Because she knew that behind the mask Carmen wore was a woman, someone passionate and real?

So who was that woman?

Amber took her glass of scotch from the table and finished it off. Now that Carmen had said yes to her, she would have the chance to find out.

CHAPTER 4

The next morning, Carmen arrived at the Pryce residence at a quarter to eight. She'd done jobs for high-profile clients before. CEOs, politicians, minor celebrities. She was used to being surrounded by wealth and glamour. But those jobs hadn't prepared her for this.

The Pryce residence was a gilded fortress, sprawled across a vast stretch of land that would be worth a fortune in this part of the city. Although the residence had probably been built years before there was much of a city to speak of. The mansion had that look about it, old, but well kept and stately, with towering sandstone walls and endless gardens.

And it was heavily fortified. Carmen had to drive through two security gates to get inside. If Amber was this well protected, what could possibly have made her feel unsafe enough to fire multiple bodyguard teams?

She made her way to the front doors of the mansion, where Wheeler stood giving instructions to the other members of the team over an earpiece.

He gave her a nod as he finished off his conversation.

"Morning, Wheeler," she said.

"Torres," he replied. "I've spoken to Pryce about how we're going to handle this. She wants your full attention on her, so I'll take care of logistics and coordinate the team as a whole. But ultimately, you're in charge here. If you need extra bodies or have any specific orders for us, we're at your disposal at all times. I've got the entire core team on this job, so you'll have plenty of extra bodies."

Carmen nodded. "Understood." The core team numbered a dozen, but there were others on call for when they needed more people.

"I'm assigning the rest of the team to positions around the residence. Hudson will be your closest contact if you need someone in a pinch." He paused. "I don't know what you did to make an impression on Pryce, but it got us this contract. You did good."

Carmen shrugged. "I don't know what I did either."

She recalled her conversation with Amber the previous evening. *You caught my attention.* Was that purely in a professional sense?

"Pryce is waiting for you inside," Wheeler said. "She strikes me as the kind of woman you do *not* want to keep waiting."

That was something Carmen had gathered about Amber already.

She pushed the doors to the mansion open and stepped inside. The interior of the house matched the outside, with marble floors, a grand staircase, and sparkling chandeliers, along with staff dressed in crisp black and white uniforms. The house was a palace, fit for royalty.

Barely a second passed before a butler approached her,

addressing her as *Miss Torres* and informing her that Amber would see her in the drawing room.

Carmen followed him through the mansion until they reached a spacious living room. The butler offered her a seat. She chose to stand instead. She didn't want to get comfortable.

She stood by, waiting. A minute passed, then two, then five. Just as Carmen's attention began to wander, Amber appeared.

She swept into the room with the same regal bearing as at the charity auction, the same manner that made everyone turn and look at her. But Carmen wasn't mesmerized by her anymore, not like she'd been that night at the auction. After their conversation in Amber's office, the woman's bossy, demanding nature had overshadowed any allure in Carmen's eyes.

So why had her heart sped up when Amber entered the room?

"Good morning," Amber said. "You're right on time."

She took a seat on a chaise lounge across from where Carmen stood, folding her hands in her lap and crossing one heeled foot over the other. In a sleek A-line dress and heels, with her elegantly styled hair and perfect manners, she was the picture of a lady.

But that was where any resemblance to old-fashioned notions of femininity ended. That intensity, that fierceness Amber was known for, radiated from her.

She gestured to the chair across from her. "Have a seat."

"I'll stand," Carmen said.

"I insist. *Sit.*"

Carmen sat. A hint of satisfaction flashed in Amber's

eyes. She obviously wasn't used to being defied. It was becoming more and more obvious that Amber was a woman who expected to be treated like a queen.

Now that Carmen was working for her, would Amber expect her to bow to her?

The butler returned, serving Amber coffee in a cup and saucer before offering Carmen refreshments. Carmen declined. She wasn't here to have tea. She was here to do her job.

Amber took a sip of her coffee before returning her attention to Carmen. "I can tell you're eager to get down to business, so let's get started, shall we? As we've already discussed, I require you to be with me at all times. I'm holding you personally responsible for my security."

"Understood," Carmen said. "And if I'm going to keep you safe, I need some information from you. I need to know all about your usual movements, your schedule, any close contacts, details of the residence's security system, and so on."

Amber nodded. "I can provide all of that for you."

"And I need to be informed of any known threats to your safety. Like this stalker."

"Ah, yes. It was only a matter of time before you brought that up." Amber set her coffee cup down in the saucer. "It's difficult to explain what's going on. All I have are some letters. And a feeling. Someone is stalking me. I just know it."

"Why don't you tell me about it?" Carmen asked. "When did you first notice that something was going on?"

"A couple of months ago, when I received the first letter."

"What did it say?"

"It's easier if I show you." Amber reached across to the side table and picked up a pile of papers. Letters. "Here. They're in chronological order."

She handed them to Carmen. Carmen scanned the first letter.

I can't stop thinking about you... I miss you. I want to see you again... I want to be with you...

"They're all unsigned, with no return address," Amber said. "And they're postmarked from various locations around the city. As you can see, the contents of the letters are overly familiar, but I have no idea who the person writing them is."

Overly familiar was one way of putting it. The letter read as if it were written by a lover, extolling the virtues of Amber in a way that felt very intimate.

"The first letter made me uneasy, but I assumed it was just from an admirer. My family is well known, so I've attracted more than one overzealous fan in the past. But this feels different. And the letters, they've become increasingly disturbing."

Carmen flipped to the next letter, then the next. They all contained language that suggested an intimate relationship with Amber. And each letter became more and more neurotic, more obsessive.

I can't get you out of my head. I need to see you again. I need to touch you, feel you. I want to explore every part of you, taste your lips, breathe your essence. I still remember the scent of you, of your hair, of your skin...

I love you. I need you...

You're my everything...

I'd give my life for you.

The rest of the letters were more of the same. One simply had the phrase *I love you* written over and over for half a dozen pages.

But the most recent letter ended with a declaration, bordering on a threat.

I'll do anything to be with you. Whatever it takes, I will be yours again.

Carmen set the letters down on the table in front of her. "I can see why you're concerned. So you don't have any ideas about the sender's identity?"

Amber shook her head. "Nothing. The letters, they're written as if the person has a history with me, but I have no idea who they are. I can't think of anyone in my life who it could be. Whoever sent these is delusional."

"So you believe they're a stranger? Not a jilted ex, a former lover?"

"I've considered the possibility, but I've spoken to every ex, every lover. They deny any involvement."

"And you believe them? They could be lying."

"No, that's not a possibility. I'm very selective about my lovers. There have been very few of them for that reason. I only enter into relationships of any kind with women who I trust. So I believe them when they say they're not involved."

It didn't surprise Carmen that Amber was interested in women. Amber was notorious for keeping her personal life private, never appearing in public with a partner of any gender. But inevitably, rumors spread. And rumors that Amber Pryce was a lesbian were rife, especially among the women of the city who were the same way inclined.

Besides, Carmen had sensed it in the way that Amber

kept looking at her, with those charged glances that made her hot all over.

Amber interrupted her thoughts. "While I'm certain it isn't anyone I've had an intimate relationship with, I do wonder if this person is close to me, somehow."

"Why is that?" Carmen asked.

"It isn't just the overly familiar letters. Lately, I've been getting the sense that I'm being watched."

"What have you noticed?"

"Nothing specific. It's just a feeling. That's why I haven't gone to the police. I have no proof, no evidence. But I just know someone is after me. And whoever it is, they've created this delusion of a relationship with me. They're obviously unhinged."

Amber was right. This wasn't much to go off of. But it was clear from the contents of the letters that the sender was unstable. And as Carmen studied Amber's impassive face, she saw something flicker behind her eyes, just like it had that moment outside the charity auction.

Fear.

Whatever was going on, Amber was afraid. And she wasn't the kind of woman who was scared of anything.

But as quickly as that fear had appeared, it was gone. "I know that I'm right," she said. "And I don't care if you believe me or not, as long as you do your job and keep anyone dangerous from getting close to me."

"I believe you," Carmen said. "And I'll do everything in my power to keep you safe. But if I'm going to do that, I'll need you to follow my directions when it comes to matters of security."

Amber gave her a stiff nod. "Certainly."

But something told Carmen that following directions wasn't something Amber was accustomed to.

"You're going to have to take some precautions until we have a better sense of the threat this stalker poses," Carmen said. "There's only so much my team and I can do. Fortunately, the residence here is well fortified. If we limit your external movements, it will be easy to keep you out of harm's way."

Amber shook her head. "Absolutely not. While I'm willing to be more careful, I refuse to stay locked up in my house. I have a busy schedule."

Carmen held back a sigh. Amber wasn't going to be an easy client. "We'll come back to that. How about we talk about what we can do to protect you here in the residence? While it's very secure, its size means that we'll need to make sure any potential vulnerabilities are covered, particularly when it comes to the parts of the house you spend the most of your time in."

"Certainly. I'll give you a tour. If you're going to be living here, you'll need to get to know the place."

"Living here?"

"Of course. You're my personal bodyguard. You're to be with me at all times, aside from your days off."

Carmen held up her hands. "Hold on. I didn't agree to that."

"It's all in the contract. I discussed it with your boss. I assumed he told you."

"He failed to mention that." Probably because he was desperate to lock in such a lucrative contract. "Look, I can rotate out with one of the other team members at night, but I can't move here."

"It's part of the deal. I want you here all the time, or not at all." Amber folded her arms across her chest. "This contract is for the next three months. Once it ends, I'll decide whether I want to renew it long-term, and we can revisit the terms. But until then, I expect you to be here, day and night."

Why was Amber so insistent on having Carmen with her? But given that the entire contract hinged on Carmen being Amber's personal bodyguard, what choice did she have? She couldn't let the team down by losing the contract for them.

Besides, it was only for a few months. She could think of it as just another tour of duty. And a very cushy one at that.

"All right," she said. "But I need to talk to Jo about this."

Amber cocked her head to the side. "Jo?"

"Joanna, my sister. I'm her guardian. She's 18 now, but I've never left her alone for long, so I need to make sure she'll be okay fending for herself."

"I understand. You have a duty to your family, and I respect that. But as soon as you've cleared things with your sister, I want you to move into the residence."

Carmen nodded. "I'll talk to her tonight."

Amber rose from her seat. "Come, I'll show you the house."

She swept off out of the room and into the hall, barely giving Carmen a chance to follow her. Carmen suspected this was going to be something she'd need to get used to.

"We'll start from the entrance and work our way back," Amber said. "The residence is quite large. It's over 350 years old, and it's been in my family for generations. I grew up here, but I only moved back in recent years when my mother moved to the summer residence. I suppose you could say I'm the mistress of the house now."

Summer residences? Mistress of the house? Amber lived in an entirely different world to Carmen.

They made their way through the house from room to room, Amber describing each one and its function. The sunroom. The drawing room. The receiving room. Carmen took mental notes on every room and hallway, memorizing any potential security vulnerabilities. The east sitting room had an entry door into the garden that didn't lock properly. The balcony off one of the upstairs guest suites was scalable, if an intruder was determined enough.

Finally, they reached Amber's personal quarters.

"This wing of the house is mine," she said. "It's off limits to the general house staff so that I can have some privacy, but a select few of the housekeepers are allowed to come and go. Of course, you'll have free run of the house, including my wing."

Carmen followed her through the door to Amber's wing, where Amber proceeded to show her each room within it.

"That's my personal sitting room, where I go when I want to relax," she said. "My study is through there. And this is my bedroom."

They had to pass through a smaller antechamber before reaching the bedroom. Once inside it, Carmen checked the windows and the balcony. They were secure. No one would be getting into the house through them.

Amber led her back out into the antechamber and gestured through another door. "You'll be sleeping in there. The room traditionally served as quarters for the handmaid of the lady of the house, but it will serve you well as my personal bodyguard. I'll have the room prepared for you."

Carmen looked inside the room. It was already well furnished enough, although not to the extent of the rest of the extravagant house.

"You're welcome to request anything specific that you'd like, both for your room and the house in general. Just let the staff know."

As Amber led her back into the hall and made to leave her wing, Carmen noticed a door right at the end of the hall. Amber hadn't shown her what was beyond it. From the mental blueprint Carmen had made of the mansion, there had to be a sizable room there.

Carmen stopped and called Amber's name.

Amber turned to face her. "Yes?"

"What's behind that door?" Carmen asked.

Amber waved a dismissive hand. "You don't need to worry about that. It's the most secure room in the house. It's locked, and only I have the key. No one sets foot in there unless I want them to."

Was it a panic room? A vault? It wouldn't surprise Carmen if the house had either.

"I assure you," Amber said. "There are no threats behind that door."

Carmen crossed her arms. "I'd like to be the judge of that."

The slightest hint of a smile crossed Amber's lips. "If you insist."

She swept past Carmen, heels clicking on the floor as she approached the door. Producing a key out of nowhere, she unlocked the door and pushed it open.

She gestured inside. "After you."

Carmen glanced between Amber and the room warily. Why did she suddenly feel like she was walking into an ambush?

Guard raised, she stepped through the door. The room was dark, but she could make out the outline of a bed by the far wall.

"I'll get the light," Amber said.

The lights flicked on, illuminating the room. Carmen froze in place. It wasn't a vault or panic room. And it wasn't a bedroom either, despite the large bed by the far wall.

No, this room had a single, obvious purpose. It was a space designed to explore every kinky, sensual pleasure imaginable. It was furnished with riding crops and canes, restraints, cuffs, and shackles, toys and tools of pleasure and pain. The walls were a deep purple, but everything else was jet black, from the silk sheets to the leather whips displayed on racks around the room. And gold accents adorned everything, from the furniture to the collection of gilded handcuffs arranged in a velvet case on a nearby chest of drawers.

It was an erotic playroom, fit for a queen.

A hot shiver trickled down Carmen's back.

Amber spoke up beside her. "Now you know what's behind this door. Any questions?"

Carmen shook her head. "No."

"Are you sure? Because a moment ago, you were so eager to see what was in this room."

Amber stepped toward her. Carmen resisted the urge to step back. She didn't back down from a challenge. But suddenly, she felt overpowered by the other woman, not physically, but by her presence, by the look in her eyes, like she wanted to pin Carmen against the wall there and then.

Carmen's heart began to pound. Amber raised a hand toward her, making her heart thump even harder.

But Amber reached around her, taking something from a rack behind Carmen's head. It was a short, thin whip, black with gold thread woven into the handle.

She drew the whip through her hand lovingly. "You strike me as the kind of woman who isn't afraid of anything. The kind of woman who enjoys a thrill."

Carmen's head grew light, filled with the dizzying scent of the leather whip mingled with Amber's sweet perfume. It was intoxicating. *She* was intoxicating.

Amber leaned in close, her voice dropping low. "Since you're so curious about this room, I'm more than happy to give you a hands-on demonstration of what goes on in here."

A sharp, hot breath left Carmen's lips. Her entire body felt like it was on fire. As she looked back into Amber's ice-blue eyes, she could feel the desire in the woman's gaze, could hear Amber's unspoken demand in her mind.

She wanted Carmen to bow to her. But not in the way Carmen had expected.

Something awakened deep inside her, an urgency, a hunger that needed to be sated…

No. That wasn't what she wanted. Those feelings, they weren't *her*.

She shook her head, clearing the fog from her mind. "I've seen enough."

"If you say so," Amber purred. "But if you change your mind, just say the word."

Carmen remained silent. A moment passed, then another. Amber didn't move. But neither did Carmen.

Finally, Amber returned the whip to its place on the rack. Then, her usual frosty demeanor returned.

"Come along now," she said. "I'll show you the staff quarters."

Turning on her heel, Amber left the room, stopping outside the door to wait for Carmen. Carmen took one last glance at the room before leaving it. As Amber locked the door, Carmen realized she hadn't checked the room for security vulnerabilities. But she had no intention of going back inside that room.

So why did she feel this magnetic pull toward it as they walked away?

And why couldn't she stop picturing Amber standing inside it, drawing the leather whip through her hands?

CHAPTER 5

That night, Carmen returned home to find her sister in her usual spot on the couch with her laptop.

"Sorry I'm so late," Carmen said. "First day at the new job and all."

Jo murmured a greeting without looking up from her screen. "It's cool."

"I'll get started on dinner."

"I already made something. Leftovers are in the oven."

Carmen went into the kitchen and served herself a plate. She didn't like how often Jo took care of dinner these days. Sure, she was just as capable as Carmen in that department. Their abuela had made sure they both knew how to cook and clean, how to take care of themselves. But Joanna was too young to have to worry about those kinds of things.

Carmen took her dinner back to the living room and joined Joanna on the couch. It was impossible to ignore it. Joanna wasn't a kid anymore.

But was she really an adult? Was she mature enough to handle the real world? It hadn't been long since Carmen had

had to confiscate her devices at night, otherwise she'd stay up late playing video games and would fall asleep in class. And when it came to getting in trouble at school, that had just been the tip of the iceberg.

Carmen worried about her. Their parents' deaths had hit them both hard, but it had hit Jo harder. She'd been too young to remember it, but she had been there, with Carmen, when their parents were killed in front of their eyes. It had been a home invasion gone wrong. Just like that, their parents had been taken from them.

And Carmen was to blame for what happened that night. She'd never forgiven herself for it.

That was why when their grandmother had been taken from them too, in a car accident, Carmen had dropped everything to take care of her. Jo had been through too much loss. She needed her big sister.

They'd been lucky enough that their parents had left them enough to get by on their own. Most of that money had gone into the house they lived in, along with Jo's college fund. And Carmen's job provided enough of an income to sustain them day to day.

But her job was only partially about making money. After leaving the Marines, she had found herself missing the sense of purpose it had given her. Her job as a bodyguard allowed her to use the strength she'd gained in the Marines to help others. But Jo had always been her number one priority, and she still was.

After eating a few bites of her dinner, Carmen set her plate down and turned to her sister. "There's something I want to talk to you about."

"I need to talk to you too," Jo said. "But you go first."

"It's about my new job. It's with Amber Pryce. She—"

Jo grinned. "I knew it! You were being all weird about it. I knew there had to be a reason."

"The reason was that it wasn't a sure thing until now. And Amber is an important person, which means you can't go telling anyone that I'm her personal bodyguard."

"You're her personal bodyguard? That's so cool. I won't tell anyone, I promise."

Carmen gave her a firm look. "I mean it. No one can know, not even your friends."

Jo nodded. "You can trust me."

"Good. And another thing. She wants me with her 24/7, which means moving into her residence for the time being."

"Does that mean I get the house to myself?"

"Yes, but I'll come check in on you now and then," Carmen said. "And I'll still get the odd day off. But what I'm trying to say is, I won't be around all the time. If you're not okay with that, I can work something else out. There are other jobs out there."

"Are you kidding? You can't turn down this job. It's for *Amber Pryce*. And I've told you a million times, I'm eighteen, not eight. I can take care of myself."

"I know you can."

"But you don't act like it. You treat me like I'm still a kid."

Carmen felt a stab of guilt. "I know. I'm sorry, I'll try to do better, okay?"

"I'm glad you said that. Because I've been meaning to talk to you about college."

"Have you chosen a school yet?" Jo had gotten offers from a few schools.

She nodded. "I've decided I want to go to Stanford."

"Stanford? But that's on the other side of the country. You'll have to move away."

"I know. I've applied for some scholarships to cover the costs, but even if I don't get them, my college fund should have enough, right?"

Carmen frowned. "Sure. But why not pick one that's closer to home?"

"Stanford has one of the best computer science programs in the world. And it looks really interesting. You're the one who said I should do something useful with my interests, so that's what I'm doing."

Jo had discovered her talent with computers back in middle school. As far as teenage obsessions went, it was unusual, and mostly harmless. But then Jo had started using those talents in rebellious ways, which had landed her in trouble more than once. The tipping point had been when she'd hacked the school district's system and messed with their records, just because she could. She'd almost ended up with a criminal record, but the school district had taken pity on her due to her family situation and the fact that she was a good student otherwise, and they'd declined to press charges.

After grounding her and taking away all her devices until she was certain Jo had learned her lesson, Carmen had encouraged her to instead use her skills to work toward getting into a good college. And she had done just that. Carmen should have been proud.

So why did she feel so uneasy about letting her sister go?

"You should think about this," she said. "You have lots of time to decide, so why rush into things?"

Jo crossed her arms. "I don't need to think about it. I've already made up my mind."

"I'm serious, Joanna. You need to think this through, explore all your options. This is a big decision. You're barely 18."

"So what?" Jo said. "You were 18 when you decided to join the Marines."

"Yes, and at 18, I was young and naïve. I don't regret my decision, but looking back, it was rash. I'm really lucky that it worked out for me. You might think you're an adult now, but you're still so young."

Jo scowled. "I knew you were going to react like this. This is why I haven't brought it up until now. But you know what? I don't even need your permission."

Carmen opened her mouth to respond, but Jo didn't give her a chance.

"I'm going to Stanford, whether you like it or not. You'll just have to deal with it."

Without another word, she got up and stormed out of the room.

Carmen sighed. She was used to Jo's moods. She would talk to her when she'd calmed down. But for now, she had other things to deal with. Like the fact that she was about to move into Amber Pryce's mansion to be her personal bodyguard.

The events of the morning flooded her mind, a scene replaying in it over and over. She and Amber, alone in that room at the end of the hall.

She closed her eyes. When she'd stood in that room, she'd felt something. There'd been a surge of adrenaline, that familiar, addictive mix of excitement and something not unlike anxiety.

And underneath it all was a simmering, smoldering desire, which had grown even more intense when Amber had reached for that whip. Just recalling that moment made her feel it all over again.

Carmen shoved the feeling down deep. She wasn't interested in what was in that room. And she wasn't interested in Amber.

Abandoning her dinner, she got up, went into her bedroom, and began packing her bags.

CHAPTER 6

A mber rubbed her temples and looked up from the
endless pile of paperwork on her desk. This was one
of those days she wished she'd listened to her mother's
advice about not having a job.

Her eyes fell upon Carmen, who was standing next to
the door to the office. Her wavy hair was tied back, and she
was dressed in a black pantsuit with a fitted white blouse
underneath. It was professional enough that she didn't look
out of place in the office, but practical enough for her to
move around in, if required. The look flattered her more
than seemed possible. Amber couldn't keep her eyes off her.

But that was nothing new. It had been several days since
Carmen had moved into Amber's residence. And while
Amber was used to having bodyguards and assistants,
housekeepers and grounds staff milling around the
mansion, Carmen was different.

Amber couldn't help but notice her presence. Especially
when she came sauntering out of the mansion's gym in her
workout clothes every evening. Having a space to work out

in had been Carmen's one request, so Amber had granted her free use of the gym. Carmen used it every single day, clad in a sports bra and a thin tank top, her bare, toned arms on display, those tight black workout pants leaving nothing to the imagination...

It was utterly distracting. *She* was utterly distracting, standing there, still and silent, in the exact same position she'd been in an hour ago. Something about her unwavering manner got under Amber's skin, in more ways than one.

Amber crossed her arms. "Are you just going to stand there like that all day?"

"Yes," Carmen said. "That's my job."

Amber waved toward a chair in the corner. "At least sit down. Relax, read a magazine."

"I can't do that. I need to be on guard."

"I doubt whoever is stalking me is going to slip past both your security team *and* the building's security." On top of Carmen here in Amber's office, several other members of her team were stationed in the lobby, while the rest were back at the Pryce residence.

"You can never be too careful. Even if you're not taking this threat seriously, I am."

Amber folded her arms across her chest. "This again?"

"Yes. When you hired me, you said you'd listen to me on matters of security."

"That was before you told me you wanted me to sit around the house day and night, never leaving." They'd had this conversation before, and it never went anywhere.

"It's for your own safety. And I never said you shouldn't leave your house at all. All I said was you need to limit your movements."

Amber gave her a sharp look. "I *need to*, do I?"

Carmen held up her hands defensively. "What I mean is, it would be sensible to limit your movements. Avoid any unnecessary outings. Coming here this morning was unnecessary. You could have worked from home."

"I haven't been into the office all week. I have a job to do, and everything I need to do it is here." Irritation rose inside Amber. She refused to be told what to do. Especially not by someone who worked for her. "And I refuse to let this stalker control my life!"

"I understand that. I really do. But right now, your safety is more important."

"Fortunately for me, I have an excellent personal bodyguard. I trust that you'll be able to keep me safe. That is your job, is it not?"

"Yes, but—"

"Then I'm sure you'll be able to handle it. And don't forget, you work for me, not the other way around." If Carmen insisted on playing the strict professional card, Amber could do that too.

Carmen pressed her lips together, resuming her silent vigil by the door. The woman was always on the lookout, always keeping up her guard. Was it because of her military training? Or was it something else?

Amber thought back to that very first day at the residence when she'd shown Carmen her playroom. The moment Carmen had walked through that door, she'd transformed into a completely different woman.

It was unmistakable, what Amber had seen in her that morning. That faint, glimmering lust that filled her eyes every time they met Amber's had flared into a raging desire.

And when Amber had picked up that whip, Carmen had practically melted.

Amber shouldn't have toyed with her like that. She knew far better than to mix business with pleasure. Playing games with the woman who was tasked with her personal safety was risky.

But now that she had seen that side of Carmen, she wanted more. She wanted to unravel all those layers of hers until she found that part of Carmen she'd caught a glimpse of that day again.

Amber leaned back in her chair, beckoning Carmen to her with a finger. "Come here."

Carmen hesitated, then stepped toward Amber's desk. Amber rose from her chair, rounding the desk to stand in front of it, bringing her face to face with the bodyguard.

She spoke softly, letting her voice fall an octave. "Are you always like this? So uptight? So on guard?"

A faint red flush grew on Carmen's cheeks. "Like I said, it's my job."

"I know, but you're only human. Surely there are times when you feel the need to loosen up a little?" She leaned in closer. "Everyone needs to let go now and then. Even you."

There it was again, that shimmer, that spark of desire in Carmen's eyes. Her lips parted, but she didn't speak. Only a trembling breath escaped her.

At that moment, one thing became clear.

Amber needed to make Carmen hers.

But before either of them could speak, there was a knock on her office door. Carmen tensed and spun around, staring down the brunette woman standing outside the glass door.

"That's just Gabrielle," Amber said. "She's the CMO, and a friend. You can relax."

But as Gabrielle entered, Carmen showed no sign of doing that. Instead, she returned to her post by the door.

"Can you give us the room, Carmen?"

Carmen opened her mouth to speak, but Amber cut her off.

"I assure you, I'll be safe in my own office. You can wait outside the door. The walls are glass, you'll still be able to see me."

Apparently satisfied, Carmen gave her a brief nod and left the room, shutting the door behind her. She took a place beside it out in the hall, her back turned to them.

Gabrielle took a seat in front of Amber's desk and crossed her legs. "Is it just me, or is it hot in here?"

"I don't know what you mean," Amber said.

"What I mean is, I'm sensing some tension, and not the bad kind. Who is that woman?"

"She's just my bodyguard."

"*Just* your bodyguard?"

Amber leaned back against the front of her desk casually. "Of course. Why would you think otherwise?"

"The way you were looking at her when she left? Normally you treat anyone who works for you like they're beneath your notice, but you definitely noticed her."

Amber crossed her arms. "I do not treat people like that. And as for Carmen, I'm just trying to be personable with the woman who's going to be protecting me 24/7."

"Personable? More like you're trying to get her into your bed."

"I assure you, nothing is going on between us. She's my bodyguard, and that's all."

"Sure. Those pictures from the night of the auction tell a different story."

Amber pursed her lips. "Did you need something?" While she and Gabrielle had been close friends since prep school, they got on each other's nerves at times. Now was one of those times. The fact that Gabrielle could see right through her wasn't helping.

"I just dropped by to say hello. I wanted to check up on you. We barely had a chance to talk at the charity auction, and you haven't been to work much lately. And now you have a bodyguard sitting in your office, along with half a dozen others in the lobby? Is something going on?"

Amber waved a hand dismissively. "It's just a minor issue. Nothing I can't handle."

"Are you sure? That's a lot of security for something minor."

"I assure you, I'm fine. I'm just being cautious. I have a lot on my plate right now, with work, and my mother."

Gabrielle gave her a sympathetic look. "How is she doing?"

"She's doing well." At least, that was what Amber was told. She still hadn't called her. She was just too busy, or so she told herself. "But that's enough about me. How have you been? I hear Chloe is moving in?"

As Gabrielle caught Amber up on her life, she found her attention wavering. She had too much on her mind. This stalker was just another thing she had to deal with.

But as always, she would handle it, because that was what she did.

Finally, Gabrielle looked at her watch. "I better get going. Will you be in on Friday? We're going out for lunch."

"I'll let you know." Amber was certain her bodyguard would consider lunch 'unnecessary.' Not that that would stop Amber.

Gabrielle headed to the door and opened it up, addressing Carmen outside. "She's all yours." She shot Amber a knowing smile before disappearing in the direction of her own office.

Amber gave Carmen a nod, silent permission for her to return to the room. Carmen resumed her watch just inside the door. Even from a distance, Amber could feel the heat radiating between them. Gabrielle was right about the tension between Amber and Carmen. It was impossible to ignore.

Would there be any harm in relieving it?

The thought was still coalescing in her mind when an intern came by pushing a mail cart. Under Carmen's watchful eye, the intern dropped Amber's mail off on her desk.

Amber set about opening it absently. None of it was important. But halfway through the pile, she reached a letter that didn't have an address on it. It simply had her name scrawled on the front of the envelope by hand.

Dread washed over her. She recognized the handwriting. It was the same handwriting that was on all the other letters the stalker had sent her. Until now, they'd all been sent to her home, by mail. But this letter had to have been hand-delivered.

Her whole body tensed.

"Amber?"

She looked up to find Carmen before her desk, concern in her eyes.

"What's going on?" Carmen said. "What's the matter?"

"This letter," Amber replied. "It's from the stalker. They were here, in the office."

CHAPTER 7

Carmen looked down at Amber. The woman's face was hard and blank, even more so than usual.

"Can I see it?" she asked. "The letter."

Amber handed her the envelope. Carmen examined it carefully. No address, no stamp or postmark. Amber was right. This had to have been delivered to the office in person.

Carmen weighed the letter in her hand. It was heavy and uneven. Whatever was inside wasn't just a letter. "I should open this for you, just to be safe. Do you mind?"

Amber shook her head. "Go ahead."

Carmen took a letter opener from Amber's desk and sliced through the side of the envelope. She peered into it. There was no letter inside. Instead, the envelope was full of pictures.

"Well?" Amber said. "What is it?"

Carmen turned the envelope upside down, letting the contents spill onto the desk. They were photos, a mix of magazine cutouts and images that appeared to have been printed out from the internet. All were of Amber.

And the pictures had been drawn on, like some teenage girl's poster collection, with jagged love hearts scrawled in the borders and around Amber's face. But the other embellishments were far more disturbing. In some of the pictures, Amber's features were scratched out, her eyes and mouth replaced with deep, ink-filled gouges in the paper. In others, doodled ropes encircled Amber's body, and scribbled handcuffs hung from her wrists. On one photo, a blindfold had been drawn, tied around her head.

Only in one picture had Amber been left untouched, unblemished. But underneath it, the sender had written the following words.

I will be yours.

You will be mine.

Carmen glanced at Amber. She was staring down at the photos strewn across her desk. Her face was still stone, but had grown pale as ice.

"This is... this is sick," she said. "Who would do this? What does it mean? What do they want?"

"I don't know, but we're going to get to the bottom of it," Carmen said. "And whoever it is that's doing this, I won't let them get to you."

But the fury blazing behind Amber's eyes made it clear that she didn't need reassurance. "They came into this building, into this office. They've crossed a line." Her fists curled on the table before her, her knuckles white. "We need to find out who delivered this. We *need* to track them down."

"We will. I'll make some inquiries, see if we can figure

out where the letter came from." She'd start with the intern who brought it to Amber's office. The poor young woman was probably just the messenger, but Carmen could work backward from her to find the source. "If we can find out when it was delivered, we can check the security cameras to see if they caught anything."

Amber nodded. "Get started right away."

"I'll get my team on it."

"No. I want you to handle this personally, understand?"

"Understood."

Carmen radioed Wheeler to send someone in to cover her post. She didn't like leaving Amber alone, but given that Amber was back to bossing her around, she'd obviously recovered from her shock.

Once her replacement had arrived, Carmen headed off in search of the intern who had delivered the letter. Unsurprisingly, the intern had no idea where the letter had come from, but a conversation with the mail-room assistant led Carmen to the receptionist in the Mistress Media lobby.

When Carmen asked the receptionist about the letter, she simply looked back at Carmen blankly. But after a few moments, her face lit up with recognition.

"Actually, I remember that," the receptionist said. "Someone dropped it off a few days ago. A woman."

"What did she look like?" Carmen asked.

The receptionist shrugged. "Pretty average. I think she had dark hair? Sorry, lots of people come in here every day. I can't remember all their faces. But I remember she seemed a little... unusual."

"Unusual, how?"

"She was kind of jumpy. And she looked out of place, the

way she was dressed and all. But I'm not one to judge, so I just asked her if I could help her. She asked me if Ms. Pryce was here, but she wasn't in the office that day, which is what I told her. She said she'd just go inside and leave something on her desk for Ms. Pryce. Obviously, I wasn't going to let some strange woman waltz into Ms. Pryce's office, so I told her whatever she wanted to give her, she could give it to me and I'd make sure Ms. Pryce got it. Then she gave me the envelope and left."

Carmen crossed her arms. "And you didn't think to tell anyone about something so suspicious?"

The woman gave her a sheepish look. "I did at the time, but I was really busy that day. I guess I just forgot about it. The letter must have gotten mixed in with the rest of the mail."

Carmen stifled a sigh. "Do you remember anything else about the woman? You said something about the way she was dressed."

"She wasn't exactly dressed for the office. She was wearing a sweatshirt with the hood pulled up, sneakers, jeans. And she had this weird necklace on. It's hard to explain, but she just seemed strange." The receptionist shook her head. "I wish I could be of more help. There's a security camera up there behind you. Maybe it caught something."

The cameras were Carmen's next step. She gave the receptionist a nod. "Thank you for your time."

Half an hour later, Carmen stood in the building's security room with Hudson, scouring tapes of the Mistress Media lobby.

Hudson grunted impatiently. "This is taking forever.

How are we supposed to see anything in these grainy videos? This security system is ancient."

"Stop complaining and pay attention," Carmen said. "I know it's a long shot, but we might find something."

"Or maybe there's nothing to find, and the client is just paranoid. It wouldn't be the first time."

"She isn't paranoid. There's someone after her." The rest of the team were only vaguely aware of what was going on. They hadn't seen the letters themselves. "We don't know how dangerous that someone is, but we need to take this threat seriously. Amber is depending on us."

"Amber? Since when do you call clients by their first names?"

"She prefers that."

Hudson smirked. "I'm sure she does."

"What's that look?"

"You have the hots for her."

She rolled her eyes. "No, I don't."

"Pretty sure she has the hots for you, too. I caught her checking you out after your workout yesterday."

"You're crazy."

"I'm serious. She's into you."

"Well, I'm not into her," Carmen lied.

"I don't blame you. That woman is ice cold. She chewed me out yesterday for tracking mud onto her fancy carpet. I felt like I was back in bootcamp." Hudson propped his feet up on the desk in front of him. "I wouldn't want to be with someone who could eat me alive. But I hear she isn't into men, anyway."

"Like you'd have a chance with her either way."

Hudson chuckled. "Ouch. I liked it better when you didn't have a sense of humor."

But Carmen barely heard him. Her attention was fixed on one of the screens before her. It showed a video of the Mistress Media lobby, time-stamped at just after two p.m. Someone had emerged from the elevator, dressed in a dark hooded sweatshirt. They paced in front of the elevator for several moments, escaping the notice of the distracted receptionist. The angle of the camera meant that the person's face wasn't visible, but their small frame suggested they were a woman. And she was holding something in her hand. An envelope.

It was her. It had to be.

After a minute or two, the woman made her move, setting off toward the Mistress Media offices. As she strode past the reception desk, the receptionist called out to her, finally noticing her. The woman backpedaled to the desk, then exchanged a few words with the receptionist. While the security cameras didn't capture sound, everything was playing out just like the receptionist had said.

Finally, the woman handed the envelope to the receptionist and walked back to the elevators, but not before glancing back over her shoulder in the direction of the offices one last time.

"We've got her," Carmen said. "Let's see if we can get more footage of her."

Hudson backtracked through the security footage, following the woman across multiple different camera feeds to the point where she'd entered the building. Infuriatingly, none of the videos caught the woman's face.

But now they had a few vital pieces of information that

they didn't have before. Whoever was sending Amber the letters was female. And she wasn't content with simply sending letters from afar. She'd tried to get close to Amber.

Was this the first time? Or had she been following Amber all along? It would explain why Amber felt like she was being watched.

"I want copies of this footage," Carmen said. "Talk to the building's security and get me everything that shows this woman. I'm going to go tell Amber what I found."

Hudson nodded. "Yes, boss. And be careful."

Carmen put her hands on her hips. "Be careful? Have you forgotten that I spent four years in the Marines?"

Hudson held up his hands defensively. "What I meant was be careful with Pryce. Don't get too personally involved with a client's drama. That's never a good time."

"I won't," Carmen said. She would do her job and keep her client out of danger. But she had no intention of getting involved with Amber in any other way, no matter how tempting it was.

Carmen finished brushing her teeth and headed back to her bedroom. As she passed through the anteroom, she glanced at Amber's bedroom door. It was shut. Amber had turned in an hour ago, earlier than usual.

Was she unsettled by the events of the day? When Carmen had shown her the videos of the woman, Amber had barely reacted other than to confirm that she didn't know her. She'd seemed completely unfazed. And she'd seemed perfectly fine when she told Carmen she was going to bed.

But then again, Amber seemed like the kind of woman who never allowed any weakness to show.

Carmen shut her bedroom door and grabbed her phone from the nightstand, sending her sister a goodnight text. Hopefully, it would remind Jo to go to sleep. She set her phone down and got into bed. But as she lay there for a minute, then five, then fifteen, sleep eluded her. While Amber seemed unaffected by the events of the day, Carmen couldn't say the same for herself.

Up until now, this threat they were facing hadn't seemed real. But those pictures, they were far more threatening than the letters, somehow. It was those doodles, those child-like scribbles of handcuffs and ropes, those gouges over Amber's eyes, that disturbed her. This woman wanted to hurt Amber. Whether or not she would act on those desires was unclear, but Carmen wasn't taking any more chances.

Sighing, she got out of bed. She would conduct a final check of Amber's wing, just to make sure everything was secure. She left her bedroom and headed out into the hall, then moved from room to room systematically, keeping an eye out for any security vulnerabilities. Every room was clear, and every window and balcony door was locked.

Finally, she found Hudson was at his post, standing outside the doors that led to Amber's wing, outside of her private sphere where no one else was allowed, but close enough that Carmen could call on him in an emergency. She gave him a nod before returning down the hall. Nothing was amiss. She'd checked every room.

Every room, except one.

She looked down the hall to the door at the end of it. Beyond was Amber's playroom. She hadn't returned to that room since the day she started working for Amber, but she'd returned to it in her mind many times since then.

Before she knew what was happening, her feet carried her to the door. As she reached for the handle, she remembered what Amber had told her. The door was always kept locked. Only Amber had the key.

But Carmen turned the handle anyway.

And the door clicked open.

Slowly, she stepped into the pitch-black room, then felt around on the wall beside her until she found the light switch. She flicked it on. The room flooded with soft light, illuminating the deep purple walls and all they held. The ropes and handcuffs, whips and riding crops, tools and toys all tantalizingly erotic.

Something stirred inside her again, a heat that rose through her body and made her skin sizzle. What was it about this room that made her feel this way? Was it because, when she looked at the whips on the walls, she recalled Amber holding one, drawing it along her palm in the most enticing way? Was it because, when she looked at the ropes, she saw herself bound up in them?

Was it because, unexpectedly, those images excited her?

She closed her eyes, letting that thrill wash through her, just for a moment.

"Couldn't sleep?"

She opened her eyes and spun around. Standing in the doorway, barely more than a silhouette in the dim light, was Amber. She wore a short silk nightgown, covered only by a sheer white robe.

Carmen's pulse quickened. "I was just checking the house."

"Ah, yes," Amber said. "Just in case someone tries to break into this room, at the back of the house, on the second floor?"

"I…"

"As I said, this room is secure inside and out. No one gets in here unless I want them to." Amber stepped inside, closing the door behind her. "There's no need to pretend. I know why you're really in here. Your curiosity got the best of you."

"No, I was… I didn't mean to intrude."

"I'm not mad. Why do you think I left the door unlocked?"

Carmen frowned. "What do you mean?"

"How many times do I have to tell you? No one sets foot in this room unless *I want them to.*"

Carmen's mouth fell open. Amber had set this up?

She sauntered over to where Carmen stood, hips swaying seductively, stopping barely a foot from her.

"You're in here because I want you here. I want *you*, Carmen. I know you want me too. And I know you want all this." Amber's gaze flicked around the room before returning to her. "I saw it in your eyes when we were in here the other day, just like I can see it now. You're dying to let your submissive side out, with me."

Carmen glanced around them. That wasn't what she wanted. Was it?

Amber spoke again, her voice smooth as silk. "My offer still stands. I can show you what it's like to get in touch with that part of yourself, to let that woman you keep hidden inside of you out, right here, right now."

Carmen's breath caught in her throat. She gazed back at Amber, at her piercing blue eyes, at her lips, so close. Amber reached for her, drawing her fingertips up the side of Carmen's arm, up her shoulder, the side of her neck, sending a shiver through her.

She closed her eyes. That image of herself, bound up with ropes, filled her head again. But this time, Amber was standing over her...

"I..." Carmen took a step back, shaking her head. "I should go."

Without waiting for a reply, she fled the room and returned to her bedroom, shutting the door behind her, breathing hard.

CHAPTER 8

A mber finished off her post-dinner drink and gave the woman sitting across from her a smile. "It's been so lovely catching up with you. When are you in the city next?"

"Not until next month," Lydia replied. "The shareholders' meeting."

Lydia was one of the executives Amber owned Mistress Media with. She'd moved to Paris to run the Mistress offices there, so it wasn't often she was around, which was why Amber was here having dinner with her, despite her bodyguard's protests.

Amber's gaze flicked over to where Carmen stood by a nearby wall, inconspicuous aside from the intense look in her eyes as she surveyed the restaurant. If Carmen had her way, Amber would be locked up in her house, safe from the claws of this mysterious stalker of hers. The woman's insistence that Amber imprison herself in her residence was only half of the reason Amber was infuriated by her.

She returned her attention to Lydia. "We'll have to do

dinner again when you return. And you must bring Kat with you next time."

"I will," Lydia said. "She was going to fly in with me this morning, but she was too busy setting up our new apartment. You'll have to come visit once we're settled in."

"I'd love that. I haven't been to Paris in years."

With a brief embrace, they said their goodbyes, and Lydia left the table.

As soon as she was out the door, Carmen marched over to Amber. "Are you done? Let's get out of here."

"Why the rush?" Amber asked.

"You know why. You're exposed here. It's impossible to keep an eye on you in a place this big."

Amber stifled a sigh. Carmen had become even more uptight since the stalker had sent those pictures. But Amber suspected her bodyguard's demeanor had less to do with that and more to do with what had happened later that night in her playroom.

Why had Carmen reacted the way she had? One moment, she'd been dissolving at Amber's touch, moments from falling under her spell. The next, she had shut down completely.

Why was she so afraid of feeling what she felt? Her submissive desires were so clear to see. Was Carmen conflicted about them? She wouldn't be the first woman to feel that way.

Or was it simply the principles of professionalism that made her hold back? After all, she took her job so seriously. She was always on the lookout, always had her guard raised. What would it look like to have her let that guard down?

What would it feel like to have her on her knees, at Amber's feet?

She shoved the image to the back of her mind. "All right. Let's go home."

Carmen gave her a curt nod. "I'll have the car brought around the front."

She spoke into her earpiece, summoning one of her colleagues with the car. They'd replaced Amber's old driver with a member of the security team who had experience in evasive driving in case they ever needed to get her out of danger quickly. Amber had wanted a security team who took her safety seriously, and that was exactly what she'd gotten.

But she'd also gotten a stubborn personal bodyguard who seemed intent on controlling her every move.

After waiting a few minutes, they left the restaurant, stepping onto the busy sidewalk outside it.

Carmen glanced down the street. "Where's Miller with the car?"

"I'm sure he's coming," Amber said. "Relax, will you?"

"How am I supposed to relax when you keep insisting on going to all these unnecessary social events? This is the fourth one this week!"

"I'll have you know, this dinner wasn't a social event. Lydia is Mistress Media's CFO. We had business to discuss, and this was the only time our schedules lined up." In truth, most of their conversation had been personal rather than business, but that was beside the point. Amber's bodyguard had obviously forgotten her place.

And she'd let it slide for far too long.

She crossed her arms. "All these comments about how I

conduct myself need to stop. Do I have to remind you who works for whom here?"

"I'm just trying to keep you safe," Carmen replied.

"So do your job and keep me safe. That's what I hired you for, not to tell me what I should and should not do. Not to control me. Or do I need to find myself another bodyguard?"

Carmen failed to hide the scowl forming on her face. "No."

"Good, because I will not tolerate another word about my personal affairs. Keep your thoughts about them to yourself."

Carmen held up her hands in conciliation. "All right. Just let me track down this car." She looked down the street. "Where the hell is it?"

She tapped her earpiece again, speaking into it sharply. Amber pushed her irritation aside. Carmen was right. They'd been standing out here for a while now, and the car was nowhere to be found.

Suddenly, her eyes were drawn to someone walking down the sidewalk. A woman. She was moving against the flow of traffic. And she was coming toward them.

Dread rose inside Amber, the same dread she'd felt that night at the gala when she'd spotted that car. And like the car, this woman wasn't stopping. She would be upon Amber in only seconds.

Noticing the woman, Carmen turned toward her. "Hey, I need you to step back."

But the woman didn't stop. And Carmen must have been off-balance, because when the woman shoved her, she fell back, slamming into the wall behind her, hard.

The woman turned to face Amber. Her head was covered in a hood, her dark glasses and black hair shrouding her face. All Amber could make out was a flash of pink lips.

Her breath seized in her chest. Who was this woman, and what did she want with her?

But before Amber could say a word, the woman stepped toward her, arms outstretched, and grabbed onto her shoulders. Amber tried to pry herself away, but the woman's grip was too tight.

She pulled Amber in close, pink lips twisting into a smile, and whispered into her ear.

"I've missed you."

Amber's stomach turned to ice. The woman spoke as if she were speaking with a lover, with affection, tenderness. It was chilling. Because Amber didn't know this woman at all. She didn't recognize her voice.

But she couldn't see the woman's face. Was she wrong? What if this twisted, obsessed stalker was someone she knew?

Suddenly, a dark shadow appeared behind the stalker. Carmen. She wrenched the woman backward, causing her to release her grip on Amber's shoulders. Thrown back by the sudden motion, Amber stumbled and fell to the pavement, her head spinning.

As she regained her bearings, she spotted Carmen grappling with her assailant. Carmen wasn't off-balance any longer. Grabbing the woman by the shoulders, she flung her to the pavement with a force that seemed impossible for someone Carmen's size. Amber's bodyguard was every bit as capable as she'd hoped. And seeing her in action made Amber's heart pound.

But as Carmen stepped toward her target, ready to pounce, the woman scrambled to her feet, stepping just out of reach. With a brief glance in Amber's direction, she took off down the street.

Carmen cursed, then hurried over to Amber. "Are you all right?"

"I'm fine," Amber replied. "Help me up."

Carmen offered a hand to her, pulling her to her feet. At the same time, a large black car screeched to a stop in front of them. The front passenger door opened and Hudson got out, looking frantic.

"Where were you?" Carmen asked.

"We got held up," he replied. "What's going on?"

"I'll explain later. Just get her back to the residence, *now*." Carmen turned to Amber. "Get in. I'm going after her."

Hudson bundled Amber into the back of the car as Carmen took off in the direction the woman had gone. But the stalker was nowhere to be seen. She'd disappeared into the thick crowd.

As the car pulled away from the curb, Amber brought up an image of her assailant in her mind. The woman's face was a blur, and it had been obscured. But there was one thing Amber had noticed about the woman, one thing she had seen clearly that had stuck in her mind. Around the woman's neck had been a thick, black, studded leather choker.

A collar.

When Carmen arrived back at the Pryce residence, it was late. Chasing down Amber's assailant had been fruitless. The city streets were too crowded, and the woman had had too much of a head start on her.

As she walked through the mansion, she ran into Wheeler, who informed her he'd been in contact with the police. While they'd taken a report, they didn't seem interested in following up on it. He'd also spoken to the owners of the restaurant in the hope of finding security camera footage, but the restaurant didn't have any cameras outside, and neither did the surrounding buildings.

They had no leads, no help. They were on their own.

Carmen headed toward Amber's wing of the house. She needed to speak to Amber, both to make sure she was all right and to question her about the woman. Perhaps Amber had caught a glimpse of her face. Carmen hadn't noticed anything that could help identify her, but she had noticed the leather collar the woman had been wearing. Hadn't the receptionist at Amber's office said something about a strange necklace?

There was no doubt about it. It was the same woman who had sent those letters, who had gone to Amber's office. The stalker.

Carmen cursed to herself. She'd slipped up. She should never have let someone get that close to her client. Would it have happened if she hadn't been distracted by their argument?

Either way, she needed to be more careful. Fortunately, her instincts had kicked in in time for her to take action, in the end. Even now, she could still feel the aftereffects of the adrenaline surge that had taken over her.

She reached Amber's wing. But Amber wasn't in any of her usual spots. Not lounging in her sitting room, not working in her study, not in her bedroom.

Finally, Carmen found her in her parlor, a room she rarely used. She was standing by the window, looking out into the garden beyond. She still had the dress she'd worn to dinner on, still had her hair pulled up neatly at the back of her head.

Carmen knocked on the door before stepping into the room. Amber tensed slightly at the sound, but she didn't move, or speak. With the room only lit by a lamp and the moonlight outside, her face was shrouded in shadow.

"Amber?" she ventured.

But she continued to look out the window in silence. Was this Amber Pryce, unsettled and afraid? Did the events of the night finally break down her impenetrable facade?

Carmen crossed the room, stopping just a few feet from where Amber stood. She opened her mouth to speak. But instead, on impulse, she reached for Amber, placing a hand on her upper arm.

Amber turned to face her, her eyes locking with Carmen's. Her heart thumped. There was a heat in the other woman's gaze, a fire so intense that it sent adrenaline rushing through Carmen's body all over again. She'd been on edge since the encounter with the stalker. And now, alone with Amber, her hand on her arm and their bodies so close, she felt that same heady thrill.

And... something else. She felt a need, a deep, insatiable yearning that matched the lust that she could see in Amber's eyes, that she could feel radiating from her like a fog. Carmen tried to push the feeling down. Her attraction to

Amber, to all she stood for, went against everything the rational part of her wanted.

But every other part of her *needed* Amber.

The woman stepped in closer to her, closing the remaining distance between them. Carmen's pulse began to race. Amber's eyes were still fixed on Carmen's. And in the dim moonlight, they shone like a blue-hot flame.

"Amber," she whispered. It wasn't a question, or a protest. It was all the desire she felt for her, concentrated into that one word, her name.

And she didn't have the chance to say another before Amber seized her by the back of the neck and pressed her lips to Carmen's in a fiery, ravenous kiss.

CHAPTER 9

The moment Amber's lips met hers, something inside Carmen crumbled.

She closed her eyes, melting into Amber, the adrenaline in her veins replaced with pure, unbridled need. Amber pressed her body against Carmen's, firm and demanding, commanding her to yield.

A tremor went through her, a thousand thoughts racing through her mind. Amber was her client. Her arrogant, stubborn, domineering client, who drove her insane every moment they spent together.

So why did Amber's kiss set her whole body alight?

Their lips still pressed together, Amber ran her hands up the front of Carmen's chest, pushing her jacket from her shoulders, and shoved her against the wall behind them.

Carmen drew in a sharp breath, heat rising within her. She grabbed Amber's shoulders, pulling her in and kissing her harder. As she slid her hands down to caress Amber's curves, Amber locked her fingers around Carmen's wrists, pinning them to the wall at either side of her hips.

Carmen's breath caught in her chest. Her lips parted, but no words, no sound came out. It was like she'd lost control of her own body, her mind.

And it felt good.

A smile grew on Amber's ruby red lips. "Ever since you walked into my playroom, I've been waiting for this chance. Waiting to see this side of you again."

She drew Carmen's hands upward slowly, holding them against the wall above her head. A flood of lust surged through her.

"And I know you've been waiting to let that side out."

"I…" Carmen couldn't lie. But she couldn't admit how much she wanted this, wanted *her*, either.

Instead, she leaned forward, her lips colliding with Amber's in a furious kiss.

But after no more than a second, Amber broke away. "You saw my playroom. And you've been working for me long enough to know who I am. You know what I want from you, what I *need* from you." She leaned in close, her warm breath and the heat of her body burning Carmen's skin. "Obedience. Deference. Submission."

She kissed Carmen again, but slowly this time, softly, enforcing restraint. And yet, it was every bit as exhilarating. As Carmen sank into her lips, Amber pressed back against her, her thigh pushing between Carmen's legs. Carmen's knees trembled, her whole body threatening to collapse under the weight of her desire. Amber's body, pinning her against the wall, was the only thing keeping her upright.

Freeing her wrists, Amber ran her hands down Carmen's arms, her chest, unbuttoning the top buttons of Carmen's blouse in one deft motion. With a feather-light touch, she traced her fingers along the swells of Carmen's breasts, then down to tease a pebbled nipple through her bra. Deep in her core, a spark went off.

"I can feel you coming unwound," Amber said, satisfaction dripping from her every word. "I'm going to take you apart, piece by piece, until there's nothing left but the part of you that needs this. Needs *me*."

Carmen quivered. She had never wanted anything more.

Amber reached down between them, unbuttoning Carmen's pants and tearing her blouse from the waistband. Then, unhesitating, she slipped her hand into Carmen's panties, sliding her fingers down between Carmen's thighs.

A whispered curse fell from Carmen's lips as pleasure pierced through her. She ground back against Amber's hand urgently. But Amber didn't need encouragement. She wasn't holding back. She glided her fingers up and down Carmen's folds, letting a fingertip graze her clit, only lightly at first, then more deliberately, stroking and swirling, working it into a swollen peak.

Carmen trembled, overcome. She reached for Amber, wanting to draw her in, but Amber only pinned her wrist against the wall again. However, it was the look Amber gave her that immobilized her, the icy glare in her blue eyes that whispered a command to her.

Bow to me.

Carmen closed her eyes, her head tipping back against the wall. She didn't try to touch Amber. She didn't try to urge her on. She let her primal impulses take over, let her body obey Amber's commands.

And as Carmen surrendered to her, Amber slid her hand down and entered her, filling her with her fingers.

Carmen let out a halting breath. Slowly, Amber began easing her fingers in and out, sending heat darting through Carmen's body. She rocked her hips, one hand restrained against the wall, the other held at her side by the firmness of Amber's gaze. Even with her eyes closed, Carmen could feel it.

She reveled in it, in Amber's passion, her intensity, in the torrent of pleasure she rained down upon her, until finally, she couldn't take it any longer.

An eruption of ecstasy went off inside her. She shuddered against Amber, straining at her hold on her wrist, straining toward her. Amber's fingers were unrelenting, pumping and driving and drawing Carmen's climax on and on, until finally, it faded into nothing.

She leaned hard against the wall behind her, her head foggy. Amber withdrew her hand and released Carmen's wrist. But Carmen kept her eyes closed. She didn't want to return to reality. It was already rushing back to her, along with the realization of what had just transpired between them.

"Oh!" A voice, coming from the doorway.

Carmen's eyes flew open. She turned to see a woman wearing the uniform of the mansion's house staff standing just outside the door holding a pile of folded towels, one hand at her chest and her eyes wide.

Carmen pulled away from Amber, scrambling to make sure she was covered up. But with her half-unbuttoned shirt and disheveled hair, there was no hiding what she and Amber had been up to.

The housekeeper's face turned crimson. "I'm sorry!"

Amber gave the woman a look as sharp as steel. It was far more effective than words.

The housekeeper lowered her head. "I didn't see anything. I'll just go." Her eyes fixed on the floor, she turned and left the room, her footsteps disappearing down the hall.

Carmen cursed and buttoned up her pants and blouse. What had she just done? And with a client? With *Amber*? She'd been so caught up in the moment that she hadn't been able to stop herself. She hadn't even considered stopping.

Why had she let herself lose control like that?

She glanced at Amber. But the woman misinterpreted Carmen's sudden change in attitude.

"Don't worry about her. Everyone who works here understands discretion." She stepped toward Carmen. "Now, where were we?"

Carmen took a step back. "Don't." She shook her head. "This was a mistake."

Amber stiffened, something flashing behind her eyes. Was it pain? Was Amber, this unshakable ice queen, hurt by Carmen's rejection?

No, it was more likely that Amber was offended by the prospect of someone not doing what she wanted. Still, the look in her eyes made Carmen's stomach churn.

She turned away, ostensibly to locate her jacket. Finding it slung over a nearby chair, she picked it up. "I'm going to bed."

For a moment, she locked eyes with Amber. Something tugged in her chest, pulling her back toward the woman, urging her not to walk away.

But she pushed through the feeling. "Good night."

Without another word, Carmen left the room.

CHAPTER 10

C armen picked up the remote and turned to her sister. "Want to watch another movie?"

Jo murmured something non-committal, her eyes fixed on her laptop screen.

"Too old for movie nights with your big sister now, are you?"

Jo closed her laptop. "No, I'm not. Let's watch something."

"It's fine if you don't want to."

Jo shook her head. "I do, really. I've actually kind of missed having you around."

"What was that? You missed me?" Carmen ruffled her sister's hair. "I missed you too."

And it was good to be home. Things at the Pryce residence had been getting tense, so Carmen had been relieved when her day off had come around. She'd offered to skip it, given what had happened that night outside the restaurant. The stalker's actions were escalating, and Carmen didn't want to take any chances with her client's safety.

But Amber had insisted. Was she as tired of the tension between them as Carmen was? Amber had made no mention of that night. She seemed to be pretending it hadn't happened.

Carmen was trying her hardest to do the same, but it was impossible when she was around Amber. She needed some space away from her so she could breathe again, sort out her head, clear her mind of everything related to Amber Pryce.

Yet here she was, still thinking about her.

There was no point dwelling on what had happened between them. It had been a mistake, a lapse in judgment. She was *not* going to let it happen again.

"Hello?" Jo said. "Do you still want to watch something?"

Carmen blinked. "Sure. Why don't you choose?"

She handed her sister the remote. Jo began flicking through the movies on the screen.

"So, how have you been doing without me?" Carmen asked.

Jo shrugged. "Fine. Like I told you, I can look after myself. And I'll be doing that when I go to college, anyway."

Carmen pressed her lips together. They hadn't talked about college again after the other night. She still didn't want Jo moving away.

Was she being overprotective? Maybe. But her sister had sorely needed Carmen's authority back when she'd taken over as Jo's guardian. After their abuela's death, Jo had gone off the rails, and it was only when Carmen put her foot down and started being strict with her that she'd been able to turn things around.

Jo needed her. And Carmen had a duty to protect her.

But that sense of duty went deeper than just their familial bond. Carmen needed to protect her in order to make up for the role she'd played in their parents' deaths.

Carmen had played out the scene from the night of the home invasion in her head thousands of times. There were so many things she could have done differently, things that would have kept her parents alive. She could have called 911, could have gone to get help, instead of freezing up.

Or, she could have just stayed silent in the first place.

But she hadn't done any of those things. Her parents had died before her eyes. And it had all been her fault.

She couldn't change the past. But she could make up for it by protecting her sister.

"You know," Jo began, "I think that me going off to college will be a good thing. Not just for me, for both of us."

"What do you mean?" Carmen asked.

"Well, with me gone, you'll be able to go live your life without having to worry about me all the time."

Carmen frowned. "Jo, you're not stopping me from living my life. You're not a burden to me. You know that, don't you?"

"I do. But I also know how much you've given up for me. Your career, to start with. And there's everything else. You don't have any friends. Not to mention, you never have girl-friends."

"That's not true."

"It is true," Jo said. "When was the last time you were in a relationship?"

"There was someone last year."

"That teacher? The two of you dated for like, a month. That was hardly a relationship."

"It didn't work out. We wanted different things."

Jo rolled her eyes. "Let me guess, she wanted something serious, and you didn't want that because you were too busy taking care of me?"

"That's not why," Carmen lied.

"Yes, it is. That's always the reason. I'm sure you don't tell the women you've dated that, and maybe you even don't tell yourself that, but I know it's true. Do you think I don't notice this stuff?"

Carmen cursed internally. She did think Jo hadn't noticed. And her sister was right. She'd neglected her romantic life ever since she'd become her sister's guardian.

But that was because she had more important things to think about. "You shouldn't be worrying about my love life, or me at all. You should be focusing on school."

"Right, so I can go to a good college? I've already done that. And you don't even want me to go to the college I want to go to."

"I didn't say that."

"It's obvious. The only reason you haven't forbidden me from going altogether is because I'm 18 now, so you can't do anything to stop me. You just love being all controlling." Jo crossed her arms. "Maybe if you got laid once in a while, you'd stop being such a control freak."

"Jo! You shouldn't be talking like that."

"Why not? I'm an adult! When are you going to stop treating me like I'm a kid?"

"You're 18. You're barely an adult." But Jo was right. Carmen was babying her. "Look, I hear you. And I'll consider letting you go to Stanford, all right? Just give me some time to look into it."

Jo huffed. "Fine."

"Now, let's watch a movie. Did you pick one yet?"

"Uh huh. We're watching *10 Things I Hate About You*."

Carmen raised an eyebrow. "Really? Another rom-com?"

"Don't pretend you don't love these. And you never know, maybe you'll learn a thing or two about how to snag yourself a hot girlfriend."

"Just play the movie before I make us watch another action flick."

"Yes, ma'am."

As the movie began, Carmen's mind wandered back to Amber. It *had* been a mistake, hadn't it? Amber was her client. Carmen was a professional. And sex with a client was definitely unprofessional.

But was that really why she felt so conflicted about what had happened? Or was it the fact that she had enjoyed it so much? She'd liked the way Amber's fingers felt around her wrists. She'd liked the feeling of coming apart with Amber's body against hers, firm and possessive. That feeling of surrender had only made her desire even greater.

What was it about Amber that turned her mind to fog and her body to liquid, that made her *want* with a ferocity she'd never experienced before? Carmen wasn't the type to turn into a quivering mess in any situation. She was disciplined, in control, at all times, in all areas of her life. At least, that had been true up until that night.

But now, she had tasted surrender. She'd tasted Amber.

And it had only made her hungry for more.

CHAPTER 11

I t was late in the afternoon when Amber arrived at the Pryces' summer residence, accompanied by a fleet of cars carrying her security team. The sprawling residence was north of the city, more than an hour from the main house.

Immediately, Carmen got out of the car and gathered the rest of the team to secure the premises while Amber waited safely inside the car. It was clear that she wasn't taking any chances.

And it was even more clear that Carmen wasn't happy about Amber coming on this overnight trip. She'd only agreed to it because Amber had told her that the purpose of the trip was to visit her mother, who was recovering from surgery.

Still, Carmen seemed to be behaving coolly toward her. Although, that was probably more to do with what had transpired between them in the parlor the other night. One moment, Carmen had been practically begging Amber to take her, the next, she'd claimed it was all a mistake.

Just recalling that night filled Amber with this prickly heat, desire mixed with irritation. Her pride had been wounded. She was only human, after all. But her frustration had far more to do with Carmen herself than her actions. Now that Amber had gotten a taste of her, she knew she needed to make Carmen hers. It had been intoxicating, to watch—to feel—Carmen crumble at her fingertips.

Amber yearned for more. And it was taking all of her willpower to ignore that craving.

Carmen appeared at the car window. She opened the door. "All clear."

She held out her hand to help Amber out of the car, presumably out of protocol. Amber took it, pulling herself up. But she didn't miss the jolt of electricity that shot between them when their hands touched. And judging by Carmen's expression, neither did she.

She dropped Amber's hand, glancing around them before calling over one of the other bodyguards to give him his orders. Amber took a moment to take in the view of the old country manor. It was the Pryce family's summer residence, larger and grander than their house in the city. Amber had spent plenty of time here as a child, but she rarely visited anymore. The fact that her mother had moved here when her health problems started was another reason to avoid it.

Carmen spoke up beside her. "Let's get you inside."

"I assure you, this level of caution is unnecessary," Amber said. "We're in the middle of nowhere. There's no one here but my mother and the house staff."

But Carmen didn't argue with her or try to order her inside. Instead, she waited patiently for Amber to comply. It seemed she'd taken Amber's comments about keeping her thoughts to herself to heart. Perhaps Amber had been too harsh on her that night outside the restaurant.

With a sigh, Amber headed up to the manor, Carmen following just behind her at a respectable distance. That seemed like an appropriate metaphor for their current situation.

But was Carmen's coldness toward her genuine, or was she simply trying to avoid temptation?

They entered the house. Amber greeted the head housekeeper briefly before locating her mother's nurse in her rooms for an update. Her mother was recovering well, the nurse told her. In fact, she was back to her usual self, ordering all the house staff around incessantly. If there was a sign that her mother had recovered, that was it.

After dismissing the nurse, Amber headed to her mother's bedroom, stopping at the door and turning to Carmen, her shadow.

"A little privacy, if you will?" Amber said.

Carmen nodded and stepped back. Amber was surprised that her bodyguard didn't attempt to case her mother's bedroom for security threats first. It seemed Carmen had some boundaries, at least.

Amber knocked on the door and waited a few seconds before opening it. Her mother sat in bed, propped up against some pillows, her eyes closed, a book lying open across her lap. Her blonde hair was graying at the roots, but she'd made no attempt to touch it up like she usually did. But the faint, pink glow of her pale skin had returned.

She looked good, given the circumstances. She was in her 70s now, having had Amber later in life. And she had a heart condition, one which had reared its head in the form of a life-threatening heart attack a couple of years ago, shortly after Amber's father's death. Since then, she'd had several close calls, along with several surgeries and long hospital stays. While she seemed to be doing well now, her outlook had been rough for a time.

Her mother's illness had been rough for Amber too, especially when it had first revealed itself. She'd lost her father, then had come close to losing her mother in the space of a few months. She was ashamed to admit that she hadn't handled it well.

As Amber approached the bed, her mother opened her eyes and smiled. "Amber, darling. You're here."

Amber took a seat by the bed. "Hello, mother. You look well. How are you feeling?"

"Better than I've felt in a long time. I'm off bedrest next week."

"That's wonderful to hear."

They made small talk, about her mother's health, about the summer house, about the main residence in the city. It was all very polite and restrained, just like all their conversations. But Amber wasn't bothered by her mother's impersonal demeanor. It was just the way the woman was. She was strict with herself, and with Amber, expecting nothing less than perfection from her. She'd long accepted that her mother wasn't the warmest of people. Her father had been the warm one.

After a few minutes, her mother changed the subject. "There's something I need to discuss with you. It's about the Pryce Foundation Ball."

"What about it?" The Pryce Foundation was a charity

94

organization that Amber's great-grandmother had started. It provided college scholarships and other support for local girls and women, and the annual ball was where the foundation raised most of its funds. It was her mother's passion project.

"I want you to run the ball this year," her mother said.

Amber blinked. "What?"

"I know it's short notice, but you won't have to do much. The planners have everything under control. I just need you to attend and play the role of host for the night in my place."

Amber shook her head. "I'm not concerned about that. I'm just surprised that you want me to do this, considering everything that happened last time."

She didn't elaborate. She didn't want to relive the shame of that night two years ago. And the look in her mother's eyes told her she didn't want to either. That night, that brief period of her life, had been the one time Amber had let herself slip up. She'd embarrassed herself and her mother, had failed to conduct herself like the perfect daughter and heir she'd been raised to be.

Her mother had never forgotten it. Neither had Amber. It was why she'd skipped last year's ball, and had been planning on skipping this one.

"That's all in the past now," her mother said. "Besides, there's no one else who can do it. My doctor doesn't want me exerting myself, so he advised that I don't attend the event. Someone will have to go in my stead."

Her mother couldn't hide the resentment in her voice. She was a proud woman. Following someone else's orders, admitting that she needed to slow down instead of powering through life at her usual breakneck pace, was obviously hard for her. Amber and her mother were far more alike than she liked to admit.

"So, can you handle it?" her mother asked. "Because if it's too much for you—"

"Of course I can handle it," Amber replied. "This is what I do, remember? Events, balls, fund-raising for charities? It's my job."

"Ah yes, your little project with that media company." The disdain in her mother's voice was clear. "When are you going to give that up?"

"For the hundredth time, I'm not going to give it up. It's my work. It's a career."

"Pryce women don't have careers. Your job is to simply be a Pryce."

Amber crossed her arms. "No, that's your job."

"But it won't always be. In case you haven't noticed, I'm getting older. I'm not going to be around forever. One day, you're going to have to take over."

"And when that day comes, I will take over. But I won't give up my job. I can do both."

"That's impossible. With your increased responsibilities, you won't be able to afford to split your focus. You need to start thinking about the family. And about *your* family. You're well into your 30s now-"

Amber let out an exasperated sigh. "Mother-"

"You're getting older. It's time you settled down."

"Not this again. I don't understand it. You raised me to be independent, to stand on my own two feet. So why do you keep insisting that I settle down?" It had gotten even worse since her father died, and her mother got sick, and the incident at the ball. In response, her mother had doubled down in her criticism of Amber's life choices.

"Because it's important. You need to find someone. A husband to have children with, to carry on the Pryce family name."

"For the last time, mother, I am *not* interested in finding a husband. I'm not interested in men."

"You're not in college anymore. These... dalliances you have with women—"

Amber scoffed. *"Dalliances?"*

"All I'm saying is, those kinds of relationships can't last forever. You need to start thinking about your future. You need a family. You need to leave something meaningful. A legacy."

Anger boiled inside Amber. "A legacy? Whose legacy is this about? Mine? Or yours? Because that's all you care about, isn't it? The Pryce family name, about having heirs to carry it on for you?"

Her mother shook her head. "I just want what's best for you. Why can't you see that?"

"No, you don't want what's best for me. Because if you did, you'd stop trying to push me to be someone I'm not." Amber rose from her seat, her fists clenched. "I may not be the perfect idea of a daughter that you want me to be, but I am still your daughter. You taught me to be proud and independent, to stand up for myself. I will not sit here while you disrespect me."

"Amber—"

But she didn't give her mother a chance to finish the sentence. She just left the room, shutting the door behind her.

She took a deep breath, then another, trying to settle the fury inside her. Every single conversation she had with her mother lately seemed to end the same way.

And every time, Amber would sweep their argument under the rug, all so that she could keep the peace with the only member of her family that she had left. But she hated always having to be the bigger person. It only made her mother's words, her disappointment in her, sting even more.

As she turned to walk down the hall, she noticed Carmen standing nearby. Amber had forgotten all about her. She quickly composed herself, but it was too late.

"Is everything all right?" Carmen asked.

"Yes," Amber replied. "Everything is fine."

"Are you sure? If there's anything I can do—"

"I said, I'm fine!"

Carmen took a step back, falling silent. Amber felt a pang of regret. The woman had only been trying to help, and Amber had snapped at her. She was constantly feeling blinded by this tension between them, this simmering, seething thing that was moments from exploding.

And she needed to deal with it before it did, one way or another.

CHAPTER 12

Carmen stood before the door to Amber's summer house bedroom. Only moments ago, she'd been in her own bedroom next door, getting ready to turn in for the night, but had found herself preoccupied with thoughts of the woman in the room next to her.

So she'd come to Amber's door, ostensibly to check on her. But in reality, she simply wanted to speak to her, to clear the air between them. She didn't know how she was going to do that. All she knew was that she had to do something.

She knocked on the door. "It's Carmen."

"Come in," Amber called from inside.

Carmen opened the door. Amber was seated at a dressing table in a short robe, taking down her hair under the light of a lamp. She shook it out, letting it cascade down her back in golden waves as silky as the robe she wore.

She rose from her seat, turning to Carmen, her robe falling open to reveal the nightgown she wore underneath. It was short, her lithe legs peering out from underneath it.

Carmen wasn't used to seeing her dressed in something so revealing, seeing so much of her. But she didn't stare. She was a professional, after all.

But that didn't stop thoughts of the night in the parlor from filling her mind.

"Yes?" Amber said.

Carmen cleared her throat. "Just letting you know I'm turning in for the night."

"All right. Good night."

Suddenly, Carmen realized that this was the first time the two of them had been alone together since that night. Consciously or not, she'd been avoiding being around Amber when no one else was around.

But now that they were alone, the tension between them was impossible to ignore.

Amber spoke, her voice smooth and hypnotic. "Is there something else?"

"I…" Carmen tore her eyes away from Amber's lips. She hadn't realized she'd been staring at them. "I just wanted to ask. How's your mom doing?"

"She's fine. She's back to her usual demanding self."

"That's good to hear." Carmen gathered herself. She shouldn't have come here, to Amber's room late at night. She was asking for trouble. "I should go, but I'll be right next door if you need anything."

Amber's lips quirked up slightly. "Anything?"

Heat rushed to Carmen's skin. "Yes. Within the parameters of my job."

"Oh, please. When you came in here, it wasn't your job that was on your mind."

"What do you mean?"

"You know exactly what I mean." Amber stepped toward her until barely a foot separated them. "Don't think I can't see what you're doing. You want me. I've known it since the moment I laid eyes on you. And when I had you in the parlor that night, it was all the confirmation I needed."

Carmen's pulse began to pound. "That was just adrenaline, and—"

"But you refuse to admit it, even to yourself. You keep making excuses, holding yourself back."

"I—"

"You're holding back," Amber repeated. "All because you're afraid of how that night made you feel, how *I* made you feel. You're this strong, tough warrior, never allowed to let your guard down. But you let your guard down with me, let me take just an ounce of control." She leaned in close, her breath tickling Carmen's ear as she whispered. "And you're afraid of how much you liked it."

A shiver rolled down Carmen's body. "That's not..." But she couldn't lie.

Amber reached out and drew her hand down the front of Carmen's chest, fingertips trickling over her skin. "You want this. Why else would you still be standing here?"

Carmen shook her head weakly. "We're not doing this. Not again."

"All right." Amber stepped back and crossed her arms. "You've obviously made up your mind. If you're certain that's what you want, then leave. Just know that if you do, that's it. We're done—once and for all."

Carmen wasn't going to argue with that. But as she turned to the door, every part of her screamed in protest.

Why was it so hard to walk away? Why was she letting Amber get under her skin, into her head, like this?

Why did she want Amber more than she'd ever wanted anyone before?

She reached the door. It was ajar, just as she'd left it. She reached for the handle, her fingers hovering above it. A second passed, then another, and another.

Behind her, Amber spoke. "Leave. Either you leave, or you stay."

Carmen's heart thudded against the inside of her chest. She closed her eyes. She drew a deep breath.

Then, she took the door handle and pushed the door shut.

"Now, that wasn't so hard, was it?" Amber stepped toward her, her bare feet hardly making a sound. "Turn around. Look at me."

Slowly, Carmen turned to face her.

"Just so we're clear, I need you to understand what I require from you." Amber reached up to cup Carmen's cheek. "I need you to yield to me, to relinquish all control. If you're not willing to give me that, this ends now. But if you are, I'm going to give you the sweet surrender you seek."

Carmen exhaled sharply, her skin prickling from the chill of Amber's icy gaze, the firmness in her voice. Why did she find the woman's coldness so enticing?

Amber trailed her hand down the side of Carmen's neck. "Can you do that? Can you let go of it all—of control, of your inhibitions—for me?"

Carmen trembled. "Yes."

Eyes glinting with desire, Amber seized her by the back of

her neck and pulled her in, their lips crashing together in a blaze of lust and desperation. As the kiss deepened, so did the hunger in Carmen's core, the insatiable need that only Amber evoked in her. Just like that night in the parlor, Carmen's grasp on control—of her body, her mind—was slipping away.

No, she wasn't losing control. Amber was taking it.

She grabbed hold of Carmen's shirt, pulling her to the bed and pushing her down onto it. Carmen let herself fall, any remaining hesitation crumbling away. All that was left was desire.

Amber gazed down at her with ravenous eyes. "Before I begin, do you have a safe word?"

Carmen shook her head.

"Let's keep it simple. Red means stop. Stop everything immediately. Yellow means slow down. There's green, which means 'continue,' but I have no tolerance for topping from the bottom, understand?"

Carmen nodded.

"Say it. I want to hear it."

"Red means stop. Yellow means slow."

"Good. Don't move."

Carmen obeyed, watching from the bed as Amber went back over to her dressing table.

"Since I don't have all my usual tools at my disposal, I'll have to improvise." She opened a drawer and dug around in it, withdrawing a pair of silk scarves, patterned in red and black. She returned to the bed, scarves in hand. "Lie down and put your hands up."

Carmen eyed the scarves, her face growing hot. What did Amber want to do with those?

"I gave you an order, did I not?" Amber crossed her arms. "Red means stop. Yellow means slow down."

Carmen didn't want to stop, or even slow down. But she suddenly found herself paralyzed.

She wasn't indecisive. She never froze up. The last time she'd felt this way was on her first parachute jump at jump school, standing at the precipice, eager and ready to step out of the plane.

But at the same time, she'd found herself seized by hesitation. Making the leap had taken all her willpower.

"Carmen," Amber said. "You have your safe words. You have the power to stop everything. You need to trust me. But more importantly, you need to trust yourself, trust what you feel."

Amber's earlier words rang in her mind. *You're this strong, tough warrior, never allowed to let your guard down.* She was right. Carmen didn't allow herself to be vulnerable, ever. But Amber was asking her to do that now, to put herself at her mercy.

And Carmen wanted to jump.

She lay down on the bed, stretching out with her head on the pillows, her arms raised. Amber took the two scarves and tied them to the bedposts at the top corners of the bed, then looped one around each of Carmen's wrists, knotting them securely.

It was done.

Carmen's pulse thrummed, lust and excitement rushing through her veins. She was bound, powerless before the woman she had sworn to protect.

And Amber looked exceedingly satisfied about Carmen's predicament.

"Miss Torres." She climbed onto the bed beside Carmen, smiling down at her wickedly. "Ever since I caught a glimpse of your submissive streak, I've been dying to put you in your place."

She ran her hands up the front of Carmen's blouse, all the way to her collar. Making quick work of Carmen's buttons, she tore her shirt open, then leaned down to speak into her ear. "I know you've wanted this just as much as I have."

She pressed her lips to Carmen's, a firm, possessive kiss. Carmen trembled, desire rippling through her. But she didn't try to spur Amber on. She didn't fight her bonds, didn't try to take control. She didn't want to do anything other than obey.

What was it about Amber that had this effect on her? Carmen had never wanted anything like this before. She'd never fantasized about being restrained, helpless, captive to another woman.

Yet here she was, losing her mind—losing herself—in Amber.

Amber skimmed her hands along Carmen's stomach, up to the cups of her bra, drawing them down to expose Carmen's breasts. She traced her fingertips over Carmen's nipples, sculpting them into firm peaks. Carmen quivered, her chest rising involuntarily, seeking Amber's touch. Amber's fingers crackled with electricity, each brush of her fingertips sending need arcing through her.

She dipped down low, her lips grazing the side of Carmen's neck. "I can feel the way my touch makes you shiver. I can feel how much you need me."

She slid her hands down to the waistband of Carmen's

pants. In the space of a heartbeat, she had them undone. She slipped a hand into them, stroking Carmen through her now wet panties.

"How easy it would be to make you come unwound right now," she said. "I haven't been able to forget that sweet moment when I brought you to the depths of pleasure."

Carmen let out a shuddering breath, anticipation throbbing between her thighs.

But Amber pulled her hand away, peering down at her with cool eyes. "But tonight, your Mistress comes first."

Without breaking her gaze, Amber threw a leg over her, straddling her waist. Shifting forward until she was level with Carmen's chest, she reached down and drew her silk nightgown up, past her hips and waist, her chest, over her head, tossing it aside. Carmen stared, mesmerized by her honey skin, captivated by her curves.

Every inch of her was bared for Carmen to see. Yet, her dominating presence made Carmen feel like she was the one who was naked.

"Are you ready for me?" Amber asked.

Carmen nodded. The woman's intentions were clear. And Carmen was hungry for her.

Amber shifted forward until her hips hovered over Carmen's head. Slowly, she lowered herself down, stopping just out of reach of Carmen's mouth. Carmen strained up to meet her, her lips brushing Amber's silken folds, slick with her arousal.

"Yes," Amber said softly. "That's it."

She sank lower, pressing herself against Carmen's mouth. Carmen slipped her tongue into Amber's slit, drawing it up and down in long, slow sweeps, eliciting a low moan from the other woman. She dipped her tongue inside Amber's entrance, darting and delving and swirling.

Amber's head tipped back, a fevered murmur rising from her. "Yes. Worship your Mistress."

Heat surged through Carmen's body. She closed her eyes, letting Amber's presence overtake her. Her scent. Her taste. Her warmth. Her low, trilling cries vibrating through the air. She lapped her tongue, tasting her, teasing her, exploring her. She immersed herself in Amber, losing herself in the other woman's ecstasy.

And slowly, Amber's moans grew louder and louder, until her pleasure reached a climax. She arched back, grabbing onto the sheets beneath her, her thighs locking around Carmen's head, holding on against the tremors racking her body as she rode out her orgasm.

Finally, Amber shuddered, then stilled. She eased herself away, drawing in deep, heavy breaths. Carmen did the same. She was dizzy, drunk on Amber.

But Amber didn't give her a moment to rest. She crawled back down Carmen's body, dragging her hands down Carmen's waist and hips. "Now it's your turn. I want to make you come undone."

Carmen's chest hitched. Bound as she was, Amber had the power to do that, to tease and touch her until she unraveled. She was already close to coming undone. All she needed was another touch, another taste of her.

Amber reached down and stripped Carmen's pants from her legs, taking her panties off with them, then pushed her knees apart, positioning herself between them. Carmen quivered. She'd never needed someone this much before.

Amber drew a hand up the inside of Carmen's thigh, all

the way to where her thighs met. She glided her fingers up Carmen's folds, circling her aching clit with a fingertip. But she didn't linger there. Instead, Amber ran her fingers down and slipped them into her.

Carmen let out a quavering moan. She was already on edge, so wet and ready, that she couldn't control her reactions.

"That's it," Amber said. "Surrender to me."

Carmen closed her eyes and began rolling her hips, slowly, in time with Amber, letting her control the tempo. And as the pleasure inside her rose, so did the intensity of Amber's thrusts, until both reached a peak.

She cried out, the spark in her core igniting a fire that tore through her whole body. Her bound hands curled, her hips rising from the bed as her climax gripped her, amplified by Amber's unwavering fingers. At the same time, Amber kissed her deeply, devouring her with her lips as she drew Carmen's orgasm out.

Finally, Carmen fell back down to the bed, her chest heaving. Her arms tingled, numb from disuse. She needed to stretch them out.

She opened her eyes and turned to Amber. The other woman lay stretched out beside her, a look of pure satisfaction on her face.

Why did she seem a little too smug?

"Can you untie me?" Carmen murmured.

A smile crossed Amber's lips. "I don't need to."

"I'm serious, Amber."

"So am I. You don't need me to untie you. You can free yourself."

Irritation spiked inside Carmen. "This isn't funny."

Amber was taking things too far... "Wait, what do you mean, 'free myself'?"

"Give it a try," Amber said.

Carmen looked up at her wrist and pulled it toward her. It took a little force, but the knot binding it slipped free. She did the same with her other wrist, releasing it from the scarf.

"You see?" Amber said. "I tied those knots so they would slip if you pulled hard enough. You could have freed yourself at any time."

Carmen's skin started to burn. "Is this some kind of joke?" That post-orgasm fog was gone now, replaced by a haze of anger. "If you were trying to humiliate me, it worked."

Amber frowned. "No, I-"

Carmen sat up and grabbed her clothes from the foot of the bed. "I should never have come here."

"Carmen—"

She shook her head and got up from the bed. "You've been toying with me from day one. I'm done being played with."

CHAPTER 13

Amber sat up in bed, watching Carmen get dressed. This wasn't the reaction she'd expected. "Will you hold on for a moment?"

But Carmen ignored her.

"Carmen. *Carmen.* Just listen to me."

"I don't know what you could say that could make this better," Carmen muttered.

"Just hear me out. *Please.*"

The anger glowering in Carmen's eyes wavered slightly. "I don't think I've ever heard that word come out of your mouth."

Amber folded her arms across her chest. "That's how serious I am right now. Just give me a chance to explain myself."

"Fine. I'm listening."

"Come. Sit with me."

Carmen hesitated, then sat down at the edge of the bed, waiting.

"I'm sorry," Amber began. "You misunderstood my

intentions. I wasn't trying to humiliate you. I was trying to teach you something."

"Well, lesson learned," Carmen said.

"I didn't mean it like that." This wasn't going well. Amber wasn't used to openly expressing her feelings. But she needed to make this right. She saw her error now, in playing a game just to make a point. She should have known Carmen would react this way.

"I didn't mean to embarrass you," Amber said. "I was trying to demonstrate something to you, to help you understand, help you feel at ease." She placed her hand on Carmen's arm. "I know how hard it is for you to put yourself in a vulnerable position. I know you find it difficult to let go of your power, and I understand that. You're this strong woman, strict and disciplined, who doesn't let anyone get past that stony exterior. I know that submission goes against how you see yourself."

The way Carmen tensed at Amber's words told her she'd read Carmen right. So why was it that Carmen felt that way?

But that wasn't important right now. "What I wanted to show you is that despite how things might appear, you're always the one in control," Amber continued. "This power exchange between us only exists because you permit it. You might be bound, or on your knees, or at my feet, but that's only because you choose to be. You have the power here, but a good Domme, one you've grown to trust, will make you forget that. But vulnerability isn't powerlessness."

She examined Carmen's face. The woman hadn't said a word, but her eyes had softened, the anger in them dissipating.

"Again, I'm sorry," Amber said. "I shouldn't have gone about this the way I did. I should have known it would bother you."

"No, I overreacted," Carmen said. "Getting defensive is always my first instinct."

"I understand. I'll be more considerate next time."

"Next time?"

Amber let out an exasperated sigh. "Oh, come on. This is the second time in as many weeks that I've made you come so hard the whole room shook. You can't tell me this was another mistake."

"I wasn't going to say that." Carmen paused. "Okay, maybe I was. Don't get me wrong. It's not that I don't want this. But our situation, it's complicated."

"It doesn't have to be. The way I see it, it's very simple. The two of us are going to be spending all our time together for the foreseeable future. We might as well have some fun."

Carmen shook her head in defeat. "Okay. But there's one condition. One thing I need from you."

"I'm open to negotiation."

"You need to start listening to me when it comes to all matters of security."

Amber huffed. "Fine. Just as long as you don't forget which of us is the boss here." She drew a hand up Carmen's arm. "And I'm not referring to the fact that I hired you."

"I'm serious. This woman, her behavior is escalating. Until we have a better idea of who she is and the threat she poses to you, you need to stop going out in public so much. No more big events, no more of these dinners, and drinks, and parties. And you can work from home."

"All right. I'll stay locked up in the house with you."

Amber leaned in, letting her lips brush Carmen's cheek as she spoke. "I'm sure you'll be able to keep me occupied."

She pushed Carmen back down onto the bed. Carmen's breath quickened. Amber felt a pang of satisfaction.

But it disappeared when she remembered the conversation she'd had with her mother earlier.

She drew back. "But there's one exception. One event I need to go to."

Carmen frowned. "Amber—"

"I'm afraid this is non-negotiable. I'm hosting it, after all. And it's important."

"What could possibly be so important?"

"It's a ball. The Pryce Foundation's annual ball. My mother usually organizes it, but she can't run it this year because of her health, so I need to take over for her."

"Does it have to be you?" Carmen asked.

"I'm the only other Pryce left. Besides, as she likes to remind me, it will be my job to take over for her soon, not just in terms of the foundation, but everything to do with our family."

"You don't sound too excited about that. Do you even want this?"

"I..." Amber sank down onto the bed next to Carmen, staring at the ceiling above. "It's not that I don't want it, because I do. But my mother, she has high expectations of me. She always has. I was born for the sole purpose of carrying on her legacy. My parents struggled to conceive, so when I came along, it was like a miracle. Since the day I was born, I've carried the weight of my mother's expectations, the Pryce family name, on my shoulders."

Amber was always expected to be perfect, not just by her

mother, but by everyone around her. That was why she understood Carmen's need to be disciplined with herself, to wear this mask of stone all the time. Amber wore a mask of her own, one she never let slip.

No, that wasn't true. There had been one time she'd failed to live up to all those expectations, one time she'd cracked under the pressure. It had been after her father died, and her mother had gotten sick. It had all been too much for her. She'd done things she shouldn't have, behaved in ways she wasn't proud of, embarrassed herself and her family.

"This is my chance to prove myself," she said. "This is my chance to make my mother proud."

"I understand," Carmen said. "I get why this ball is important to you, and I won't stop you from going. But you don't need to prove yourself to anyone. I'm sure your mother is proud of the daughter she raised."

Amber scoffed. "That couldn't be further from the truth. She sees me as a disappointment because I haven't gotten married and had children. Sometimes I think settling down wouldn't be so bad, but my mother, she's so obsessed with the idea. And there's the fact that she still expects me to marry a man even though I came out to her when I was fifteen."

She shook her head. "Family, duty, legacy. It's all she cares about. I'm so tired of it. But at the same time, I love her. I'm all she has left, and she's all I have left."

"I understand that," Carmen said. "Family is important."

Amber turned her head to study Carmen's face. Her expression had grown wistful. "You have a sister, don't you? Joanna?"

"You remembered that?"

"Of course. You're her guardian?"

Carmen nodded. "She's 18 now, so I suppose she doesn't need one anymore, but I've been taking care of her for almost five years now. Our parents died when we were young, so our grandmother raised us until she passed too. I'm all Jo has."

"I'm sorry," Amber said. "It must have been difficult losing your parents so young. And your grandmother too."

"It was, but we had each other. I just wish my sister hadn't had to grow up without parents. Their deaths were so senseless. And I should have saved them..." Carmen shook her head. "But the past is in the past."

Carmen felt silent. Amber draped an arm around her, pulling her close. She obviously didn't want to talk about things any further. But Amber couldn't help but wonder about what it was that Carmen found too painful to talk about.

I should have saved them.

What did that mean?

CHAPTER 14

The next day, Amber said a tense farewell to her mother before seeking out Carmen to inform her she was ready to leave. She found her bodyguard in the living room at the front of the house, staring out the window, presumably looking for any signs of trouble.

"There you are." She entered the room and strode over to where Carmen stood.

Carmen gave her a stiff nod. "What can I do for you?"

Amber smiled seductively. "I can think of several things you could do for me, each one wickeder than the last." She stepped in close, speaking softly. "And now that I have you alone, we can finally do them."

Carmen's lips parted, the faintest of breaths escaping them. She glanced around furtively. "Someone could see us."

"Would that be so bad?"

"Yes, it would. We agreed, remember?"

Before Carmen returned to her bedroom the night before, the two of them had agreed that unless they were sure they were alone, they would behave as if nothing had changed in order to keep their affair under wraps. It wasn't easy, considering that every time their eyes met, all Amber could think about was dragging Carmen into the nearest room, shutting the door, and kissing her up against it.

"If my colleagues saw us together, I'd be in so much trouble," Carmen said. "Not to mention, I'd never live it down."

"They're just jealous." Nevertheless, Amber took a step back. "I'll try my best to keep my hands off you, for now. But as soon as I get the chance, I'm sneaking you into my playroom back at the house so I can finally give you that demonstration I owe you."

Carmen's face flushed ever so slightly. Amber smiled. Was there anything more satisfying than making this tough, strong woman blush?

"Ms. Pryce?"

Amber turned to see one of the housekeepers hurrying toward them. She stifled a sigh. It was like all the housekeepers were conspiring to interrupt them.

"I'm so sorry to disturb you," the housekeeper said. "Your mother left this for you the other day. I forgot to give it to you."

She held out an envelope. Amber's name was written on the front, just her first name. But while the handwriting was familiar, it wasn't her mother's.

Her heart pounding, she snatched the envelope from the woman. *How? How did this get here?*

Carmen spoke beside her. "Amber? What's the matter?"

"Where did you find this?" Amber said to the housekeeper. "Tell me!"

The woman flinched. "In your bedroom, on the dresser.

I was preparing your rooms for your visit and I put it aside while I was cleaning. I meant to put it back, but I forgot. I didn't read it, I swear!"

"Why did you say it's from my mother?"

"I just assumed. Who else could it be from?"

"This is *not* my mother's handwriting," Amber snapped.

"I-I don't understand…"

Amber turned to Carmen, who nodded.

"You're right," she said. "It's the same handwriting."

Amber flipped the envelope over and opened it. Once again, there wasn't a letter inside. Instead, there were photos of Amber. But this time, they weren't magazine clippings or pictures printed from the internet. They were candid photographs, shot and developed from film.

Amber took them out of the envelope and began flipping through them. They showed her going about her day from a distance. There were photos of her entering and leaving her office building. Photos of her at various venues and restaurants, getting in and out of cars. There was one photo that had been taken outside the restaurant she'd gone to for dinner that night when the woman in the collar had grabbed her. She'd photographed Amber going inside, and she'd waited for her to come out. How long had the woman been following her?

Was she watching Amber's every move?

Carmen was right. She needed to be more careful about her movements.

She flipped through the rest of the pictures. They were more of the same. But when she reached the final photo, her heart stopped.

Unlike all the others, the photo wasn't of her. It was of

her mother, lying in her bed here in the summer house, asleep.

Amber's hands began to tremble, shock and fury clouding her vision. The woman, the stalker, had gotten inside the house, gotten to her mother.

How had she done it? Had she hurt her? *My mother…*

"Amber," Carmen said. "Look at me."

Amber blinked. Carmen had her by the shoulders and was staring hard into her eyes. Amber had been so consumed by her anger that she hadn't even noticed.

"Everything is going to be okay," Carmen said. "I've ordered a search of the house and I'm having the staff gathered to be questioned. We're going to get to the bottom of this."

Amber nodded. She was *not* going to let this stalker get to her.

Pulling herself together, she turned to the housekeeper, who was standing by looking equal parts confused and terrified.

"You," Amber said. "Find me the head housekeeper and bring him to me. I need to speak with him immediately."

The woman nodded and scurried off. For a moment, Amber considered if the woman herself was the culprit, but given that she was half Amber's size and pushing 60, it was unlikely. But if any of the staff had anything to do with this, the head housekeeper would know.

Five minutes later, Amber and Carmen stood looking down at him as he sat stiffly in a chair. Amber explained the situation to him, showing him the picture of her mother. The man had been overseeing the house staff for over 20 years. He knew everything that went on in the residence.

But he just shook his head. "I don't know who could have done this. No one has set foot inside the house in the past few weeks other than the long-term staff. We had a plumber come in to fix some pipes in the basement the other day, but I was with him the entire time."

Amber let out a frustrated sigh. They weren't getting anywhere.

"But there was that nurse who came last week," he said. "The temp."

Amber tensed. "A temp?"

The man nodded. "Your mother's nurse was sick, so the agency sent someone else."

"And you didn't think to tell me this?"

"I didn't think it was worth bothering you about something so minor."

Amber cursed. "This nurse. Was she a woman?"

"Yes. She was young, maybe 30 or so."

Amber turned to Carmen, who nodded in silent agreement. It had to be her.

"Looks like we have a lead." Carmen addressed the housekeeper. "I need her name, along with everything you know about her."

He nodded. "I don't remember much about her. She was only here for a few hours. And I only saw her for a moment."

The housekeeper did his best to describe the nurse. Her dark hair, her age and build, all fit the description of the woman, but it was so vague that it could have described anyone. By the time Carmen was done questioning him, they had little information that could help them.

After dismissing the housekeeper, Amber turned to

Carmen. "I need you to look into this nurse. The agency should have some information about her."

Carmen nodded. "My thoughts exactly. I'll get the others to question the rest of the staff too, see if they remember anything about her." She paused. "How are you doing? Are you all right?"

"I'm fine. I'm more concerned about my mother. I can't believe I put her in danger like this."

"*You* didn't do anything. None of this is your fault. You can't blame yourself for the actions of some crazed stalker. And she didn't do anything to your mother. She didn't harm her."

"That we know of. I need to talk to her, make sure she's safe…" Something stabbed inside Amber's stomach. "We can't leave today. We have to stay here."

Carmen put her hand on Amber's shoulder. "I know you're worried about your mom, but that isn't an option. This place isn't as well protected as the main residence. The stalker already got in here once. It's not safe."

Amber's hands curled into fists at her sides, her fingernails digging into her palms. "It's not safe? And you want me to just leave my mother here, alone?"

"You're the one who is at risk here, not her. If this stalker wanted to hurt her, she would have done it already. She's trying to get to *you*. Staying here just makes you an easier target."

Amber bit back a curse. Once again, Carmen was right. But she couldn't abandon her mother.

"How about this?" Carmen said. "I'll talk to Wheeler and we'll come up with a plan to make sure this residence is secure. We can put a team here, install cameras, the works.

Your mother will be safe. And you'll be safe too, back in the city."

Amber crossed her arms. Carmen's plan made sense, but it did little to settle the unease seething inside her. "Fine, but I want everything taken care of today. The security team, the cameras. Money is no obstacle. Just get it done. We're not leaving here until then."

~

By the time they arrived back at the main residence, night had fallen. Despite her exhaustion, Amber felt none of the relief that returning home should have given her.

As she and Carmen reached Amber's wing, the bodyguard spoke up. "I'm sorry we don't have any leads. I can't believe that temp agency is so careless about who they hire."

"My mother certainly won't be using them again," Amber said. It turned out the 'nurse' had signed up for the agency under a false name, complete with fake credentials. They hadn't been able to trace her. They were back to square one.

"Even though that was a dead end, we're going to figure this out. Everything is going to be okay."

"Is it? This woman, she created an entire fake identity just so she could get to me through my mother. That's insane. That's *unhinged*."

Her stomach churned. The woman was more than persistent, more than obsessed. They weren't dealing with some overly enthusiastic admirer. They were dealing with someone willing to go to extremes, someone dangerous.

"I know," Carmen said. "But we're not going to let her get to you."

But why did the woman want to get to her so badly in the first place? Who was Amber to her? Had she been wrong when she'd dismissed the stalker as a stranger? What if it was someone she knew, someone in her life?

The woman wore a collar. And then there were the pictures of Amber she'd sent, with scribbled drawings of handcuffs and blindfolds and chains. What if they weren't a threat, but a reference to an intimate part of Amber's life, one she kept private?

What if they were both, and the woman wanted to cause her pain in a way she knew would cut Amber deep?

She shook her head. "This stalker wants to hurt me. That's bad enough. But to hurt those I love…"

Carmen took Amber's hands in hers. "I'm not going to let anything happen to your mother. And I am not going to let anything happen to you. Until we have this figured out, I'm not leaving your side. I'll stop at nothing to keep you safe."

Amber looked back into Carmen's eyes. The resolve in them was unwavering. It was clear that she was committed to her job, to protecting Amber. Was she this dedicated to all her clients?

Regardless, Amber believed her when she said she would stop at nothing to keep her safe.

But would that be enough?

CHAPTER 15

Carmen was lounging in the living room near the front of the Pryce residence when the butler appeared in the doorway.

"Miss Torres," he said. "Miss… Torres has arrived."

Carmen stood up. "Thanks, send her in."

But Jo paid no mind to etiquette, bursting into the room and nearly knocking the butler over in the process.

"Oh my god," she said. "This place is awesome."

"Good morning to you too," Carmen said.

She still thought that inviting Jo here, mixing her two worlds like this, was a bad idea. But Amber had insisted. She was the one who had ordered Carmen to take a day off in the first place. After the events at the summer house, Carmen had refused to leave Amber unprotected. But she'd barely had any time off in weeks, and it had been too long since she'd seen her sister in person. They'd eventually come to a compromise when Amber had suggested that Jo visit the residence so that Carmen could spend time with her.

Carmen gave the butler an apologetic nod. "Thanks, I'll take it from here."

As soon as he left the room, Jo let out a squeal. "Is that a butler? Does he bring you whatever you want? Can he bring us food? Drinks?"

"Yes. Yes, but I don't take advantage of the staff unless I really need something. Yes, we can get food and drinks, but no, you can't have alcohol."

Jo grinned. She obviously didn't mind the change in plans. Amber had given them free run of the house and had told Carmen that her sister could do and have whatever she wanted. It was sweet of Amber, but Carmen didn't want to exploit her hospitality.

"Now, we have a whole day ahead of us," she said. "What do you want to do?"

"Hm…" Jo crossed her arms, thinking. "You said there's a pool, right?"

Carmen nodded.

"Then let's go for a swim. And is Amber around? Do I get to meet her?"

"She's here, but I don't want to disturb her. Come on, I'll show you the pool."

Half an hour later, Carmen sat by the pool, watching her sister float around. Although she didn't plan to join her sister, she'd thrown on her swimsuit under a pair of denim shorts. She'd let her hair down too. She spent all her days in her 'uniform' of a pantsuit to match Amber's unofficial dress code, so wearing something more comfortable was a refreshing change.

Carmen watched her sister with a smile. Aside from their occasional movie nights, she and her sister rarely hung out like this. It reminded her of a simpler time, when they were younger and living with their abuela.

Of course, even back then, they had hardly been carefree. They'd both felt the weight of their parents' deaths. Jo had barely been old enough to remember her parents, but Carmen didn't know if that made it easier for her, or harder.

Carmen was grateful that she remembered them, but she'd been young when they died, barely in her teens. And she felt the weight of their deaths even more on account of the role she'd played in them.

This was why she was so protective of her sister. Carmen had failed her back then, on that fateful night. She wasn't going to fail her again. She needed to make sure her sister was taken care of.

Jo swam up to where Carmen sat and surfaced from the water. "Are you sure you don't want to get in?"

Carmen nodded. "I'm just going to sit here and enjoy the sun."

"Suit yourself." Jo let out a blissful sigh. "I can't believe you get to live here."

"It's only temporary. Until this job is over."

"Still, this place is amazing. And you get to spend all your time with Amber Pryce. What's she like?"

"You know I can't talk about my clients. All I can say is there's a lot more to her than what's on the surface. She's every bit as fierce as people say she is, but she has a thoughtful side too."

However, her sister's attention was elsewhere. She was looking past Carmen toward the house.

Carmen turned to see Amber striding toward them. As

always, she was dressed elegantly, even though she was staying home all day. Her stylish blue dress and heels were simple by her standards, but not by anyone else's. She looked as alluring as ever.

Carmen got to her feet as Amber reached them.

"Good morning." She gave Carmen a nod before turning to her sister. "And you must be Joanna."

Her sister nodded. "But everyone calls me Jo."

"Lovely to meet you, Jo. Do you mind if I borrow your sister for a moment?"

"Sure, go ahead."

"We'll be right back," Amber said. "And if you need anything at all while you're here today, just ask the staff."

Carmen gave her sister a sharp look. "No alcohol, Jo."

Jo rolled her eyes. "I know."

Carmen headed toward the house with Amber. It was only after they were inside that Amber spoke.

"Your sister is just delightful, isn't she?"

"I don't know where she gets it from," Carmen said. "I wasn't like that at her age. So, was there something you needed?"

"Perhaps I just wanted to tell you how ravishing you look." Amber's eyes flicked down her body, taking her in. "I like seeing you like this. Laid back. Relaxed. And I was beginning to wonder if you ever wore anything other than suits and gym clothes. Not that I'm complaining about those either. You look delectable no matter what you're wearing."

Carmen glanced around self-consciously. They were alone, but given the number of times that the house staff had almost walked in on them, she wasn't taking any chances.

Still, she couldn't help but push Amber's buttons, just a little. "Is that all, Ms. Pryce?"

A slight smile crossed Amber's lips. "No, that's not all. I've decided that tonight, after everyone else has gone to sleep and we have a little privacy, I'm going to finally take you into that room of mine."

Carmen hadn't forgotten about Amber's offer. More than once, she'd peeked into that room at the end of the hall, ostensibly in the name of security. Amber had stopped locking it. Carmen knew she was being manipulated, but she didn't care.

"Unless you have other plans for your night?" Amber said. "It is your day off, after all."

Carmen shook her head. "No, Ms. Pryce. I'm all yours."

"Good. And don't call me Ms. Pryce. It's much too stuffy. You may call me *Mistress Amber*."

Carmen's face grew hot. She was *not* calling Amber that. Then again, Amber had a way of making her behave in ways that were completely out of character for her. Everything about this fling of theirs was completely out of character.

"I'm sure your sister is eagerly awaiting your return. Enjoy the rest of your day with her." She reached out and tucked a lock of Carmen's hair behind her ear. "And wear your hair like this tonight. I like it this way."

Without a further word, she turned and swept away.

Carmen took a few breaths, composing herself, before returning outside. She found Jo lounging on a deck chair by the pool. Somehow, in the short time Carmen had been gone, her sister had acquired drinks.

"Don't worry," Jo said, handing her one. "They're mocktails."

Carmen took the drink and sat down next to her. As she sipped it, Jo eyed her curiously.

"Everything okay?" Carmen said.

Jo nodded. "Are we not going to talk about that?"

"About what?"

"About Amber! And you!"

"I don't know what you're talking about."

Jo raised an eyebrow. "Seriously? I saw the way you two were looking at each other. She's totally into you."

"No, she's not."

"Yes, she is. Why are you in denial about it? She's a babe."

"We are *not* having this conversation," Carmen said.

"So now you don't want to talk about her? She's all you ever talk about these days."

"I don't talk about her. I talk about my job, which just happens to be guarding her."

"You never talked about any of your old jobs this way," Jo said. "Admit it, you like her."

Carmen sighed. She wasn't getting into an argument with her sister about this. And she certainly wasn't going to tell her the truth. "So maybe Amber isn't like my other clients. We spend a lot more time together since I'm her personal bodyguard. But that's all. There's nothing else going on."

"Uh huh. That's too bad. You'd make a really cute couple."

Carmen shook her head. "You watch too many rom-coms."

While her sister had obviously picked up on the fact that something was going on between Carmen and Amber, that 'something' was nothing more than a little fun. Their entire relationship consisted of Amber threatening to do all kinds of kinky things to her until she finally gave in to temptation.

But after that night at the summer house, Carmen had begun to wonder if there was something more there, if their connection, that inexorable pull that kept drawing them back to each other, ran deeper than just their physical desires. That night had changed the way she saw Amber entirely.

You find it difficult to let go of your power, Amber had said. *Submission goes against how you see yourself.*

How had Amber known how Carmen felt? How had she seen this when Carmen herself had refused to acknowledge it? Amber understood her. From the very beginning, Amber had seen through her, seen that hidden side of herself that even she hadn't known existed.

Was that why Amber had pursued her so relentlessly? Because she saw the challenge that was conquering Carmen, getting her to give in? After all, she was a woman with enough money and power to have anything she wanted. She could easily find herself the perfect submissive, someone who would bow to her without hesitation. And yet, she wanted Carmen, a woman who had, at first, wanted nothing to do with her, or her kinky games.

'Mistress Amber' was a real mystery. But perhaps tonight would illuminate who she really was and what she wanted.

CHAPTER 16

T hat night, Carmen waited in her bedroom for 10 p.m. to arrive. That was when the house went to sleep, when everyone turned in for the night and all the staff knew not to disturb their mistress.

And that was when Carmen would meet Amber in that room at the end of the hall.

That room, behind that door, was what had set everything between them in motion. It had haunted Carmen's thoughts since the day she'd set foot in the house, consumed her mind almost as much as Amber herself had. And all this time, it had loomed there, tempting Carmen with everything it contained.

So why did the thought of walking into it, into Amber's den, scare her almost as much as it excited her?

You're this strong woman, strict and disciplined, who doesn't let anyone get past that stony exterior.

Amber had her all figured out. Carmen never allowed herself to let down her guard. But Amber required her to do that. She *demanded* it.

But Carmen couldn't pretend that she had no choice in the matter. She wanted to give Amber control as much as Amber wanted to take it. She wanted to let go, to lose herself.

And if there was anyone to do that with, it was Amber. Amber understood her, understood what Carmen wanted. Earlier in the evening, they'd talked about everything—limits, safe words, boundaries—in preparation for tonight. It had been the reminder Carmen needed that regardless of what transpired in that room, she still had her power.

Vulnerability isn't powerlessness.

Her watch beeped. It was 10 p.m.

Here goes nothing.

She left her room, making her way to the door at the end of the hall. It was ajar. She pushed it open.

Too late, she wondered if she should have knocked first. After all, 'Mistress Amber' required deference. This wasn't a great start to Carmen's attempt at letting go of control.

But the thought, along with all others, evaporated from her mind when she saw Amber by the bed. Dressed in royal purple lingerie underneath a short, sheer robe, Amber stood tall, displaying the same confidence as when she wore formal gowns and dresses. No, somehow she was even more commanding in nothing but silk and lace. With her skin bared and her feet adorned in gold stilettos, her long hair flowing down her shoulders, she looked even more like a queen than the day Carmen had met her.

"Ten p.m.," Amber said. "And not a moment later."

Only then did Carmen notice what Amber was holding —a coil of rope in her left hand and a short black flogger with threads of gold woven into the handle in her right.

Amber placed the rope on the bed where a second coil already lay, unwound, then set the flogger on the nightstand beside a trio of thick red candles, waiting to be lit.

"Come in," she said. "Come to your Mistress."

Carmen stepped into the room, shutting the door behind her, and took her place in front of Amber.

She reached up to stroke a lock of Carmen's hair. "You wore your hair down. Good. I like it this way. I like *you* this way." She drew her hand down the side of Carmen's neck, down to the front of her blouse. "All this needs to come off. I want to see you."

Carmen began to undress, stripping off the jacket she'd thrown on to keep the drafty mansion air at bay.

As she reached down to remove her top, Amber stopped her. "No. I want to unwrap you myself."

She took the hem of Carmen's blouse and pulled it over her head, tossing it aside. Then, she slid her hands down to unbutton Carmen's pants, drawing them down her hips until they fell to the floor.

Carmen pushed them aside with a foot, her anticipation growing. Amber reached around Carmen's back to unclip her bra, then slid her hands up to her shoulders and drew the straps down, one after the other, sending goosebumps spreading along her skin. Once her bra was off, Amber added it to the pile on the floor, then skated her hands down to Carmen's waist, down to where her panties sat at her hip bones.

Carmen's breath quivered. Amber's touch on her skin, her body so close, ignited a fire inside her. Her eyes were drawn down to Amber's body. Close up, she could see that the bra and panties Amber wore were

just as sheer as her robe, little more than lace adorn-
ments on her bare skin. The suggestion of nakedness
was even more enticing than if she was wearing nothing
at all.

Amber drew Carmen's panties down her hips, letting
them fall to her ankles. Carmen stepped out of them
obediently.

"There." Amber reached out and traced her fingertips up
the hollow of Carmen's throat. "Now I can really see you.
All of you."

Carmen trembled. Despite Amber's words, she wasn't
looking at Carmen's body. Instead, she stared deep into her
eyes, her gaze piercing.

What did Amber see when she looked at her? Could she
see how Carmen hungered for her? Could she see the battle
Carmen fought in her mind, between wanting to maintain
control and wanting to give it up? Could she see how
Carmen secretly yearned for her to take that control away,
to end that battle for her, once and for all?

Could she see how conflicted Carmen felt about those
desires?

Amber's voice interrupted her thoughts. "Do you
remember what I said to you that night in the summer
house? About trust?"

Carmen nodded. "That I need to trust you. And I need to
trust myself."

Amber cupped Carmen's chin in her hand. "So get out of
your head. Be here, with me."

She brought her lips to Carmen's, kissing her soft and
slow. Carmen dissolved against her, surrendering to her
tender but insistent touch. That was what her body, her

instincts, told her to do. She needed to trust them instead of listening to the fears in her mind.

And she needed to trust Amber.

Breaking the kiss, Amber drew her over to the bed, then opened the top drawer of the nightstand and withdrew something from it. It was a blindfold made of black leather.

Amber held it up before her. "Remember. Red means stop. Yellow means slow down."

Carmen nodded.

"Don't just nod. Tell me that you understand. And I believe we've spoken about how you're to address me?"

Carmen's cheeks flushed with heat. "I understand... Mistress Amber."

She barely caught a glimpse of Amber's satisfied expression before she raised the blindfold to Carmen's eyes, fastening it around her head and buckling it shut. It was a tight fit, seeming to mold to the contours of her face. When she opened her eyes, not a single ray of light reached them.

Her pulse sped up, her adrenaline spiking. Her instincts had always been highly attuned to danger, even before she joined the Marines. And right now, alarms were going off all over her body.

But she leaned into it, savoring the thrill, letting it wash over her like rain.

"Give me your hands," Amber said.

Carmen obeyed. Amber brought Carmen's wrists together, winding the rope around them and securing it with a knot. Then, she directed Carmen to the bed and ordered her to lie down on it.

Carmen climbed onto the bed, feeling her way up it with bound hands, and stretched out on her back.

"Not like that," Amber said. "On your stomach."

Carmen turned over. Then, Amber's hands were at her wrists, pulling the rope binding them upward.

Was Amber tying her to the bed frame? Carmen cocked her head, listening, but all she could make out was the faint swish of ropes.

After a moment, Amber's weight shifted down the bed, then settled near Carmen's feet. Drawing Carmen's ankles together, she bound them to each other with the other piece of rope. Then, Carmen felt the pull of the rope, downward this time. Amber was tying her ankles to the foot of the bed, just like she'd tied her wrists to the bedhead.

Carmen drew in a breath, silencing her nerves, instead focusing on the flame of desire inside her. Being blindfolded, restrained, under Amber's complete control, was only making it grow.

She trailed her fingers up the back of Carmen's leg, from her ankle to the top of her thigh, and up the length of her back. "Once again, you didn't even try to test your restraints. Your inner submissive is just that acquiescent."

Heat rose to Carmen's skin. Once again, she'd accepted her situation without questioning it. She pulled at the ropes with her arms and legs, gently at first, then as hard as she could. But they were firmly anchored to the bedframe.

"I assure you, the knots are very, very real this time. You couldn't escape them even if you wanted to. You're truly at my mercy now." Amber leaned down, her lips brushing Carmen's ear as she whispered. "You're mine to command. I'm yours to worship."

Carmen's breath caught in her chest. She reminded

herself that she was in control, that everything that was transpiring was because she allowed it.

But it didn't feel that way. Amber was making her feel powerless.

And that powerlessness was intoxicating.

"How I've waited for this day," Amber said. "To have you in this room, laid out before me, my prized possession. The fact that it took so long to coax you in here makes this so much sweeter."

Something skimmed down Carmen's back, soft and feathery, but leathery smooth. She tensed. It had to be the flogger.

Amber drew it down lower, skating it along Carmen's bare ass and thighs. "If you haven't figured it out by now, I'm accustomed to getting what I want." Her voice was firmer now, and cold as frost. "Tell me that I can't have something, and I only want it more."

Without warning, Carmen felt the slap of the flogger's tails against the backs of her thighs, like a shock of cold water against her skin. She jolted, sucking air through her teeth.

Amber dragged the flogger up the inside of Carmen's thigh, letting its tails trail between her legs. Pleasure rippled through her.

"And you?" Amber said. "You were forbidden in so many ways. I had to have you. But you were determined to resist what you felt for me."

She struck Carmen across her thighs, harder this time. Carmen gasped, the impact resonating through her. Amber wasn't holding back. She brought the flogger down again, once, twice, three times, with ever-increasing force.

Carmen hissed. While the flogger's tails stung, each strike sent adrenaline crackling through her in the most electrifying way. And deep in her core, the fire raged.

"But I knew that was just a front you put up," Amber said. "I knew what you really wanted. You hid it well, but I could see it. You wanted to know what it felt like to submit. And I knew that I had to be the one to show that to you."

She brought the flogger down, over and over, striping every inch of skin from the bottom of Carmen's thighs to the top of her ass cheeks. Carmen bucked uncontrollably. Every crack of the whip was a spark that lit up her whole body.

Finally, Amber stopped. As the stinging dissipated, she felt her Mistress's hands on her smoldering skin, cool and delightfully soft. And with every sweep of her fingers, they crept closer and closer to where Carmen's thighs met...

But at the last moment, Amber pulled away.

Carmen groaned. Hot and cold, push and pull, pleasure and pain. That was Amber all over. And it drove her wild.

"Did you think I was done toying with you already?" Amber said. "That was just the warm-up. Now I can get started."

She shifted on the bed again, then disappeared from Carmen's awareness completely. Carmen slowed her breaths, focusing her hearing.

There. Amber was beside the bed, moving something around on the nightstand. Then, a familiar scratching sound rasped by Carmen's ear, a sharp scent filling the air at the same time. It was the smell of smoke from a lit match.

The candles. She'd spotted them earlier, sitting on the nightstand next to the bed.

And she was certain they weren't just for atmosphere.

Amber's voice broke through the darkness. "This is fitting, isn't it? You and I, playing with fire? But you're a woman accustomed to danger."

Playing with fire was exactly how Carmen felt whenever she and Amber were together. The two of them were tempting fate with this forbidden, twisted affair of theirs, all under the shadow of the mysterious threat that had brought them together.

"So, do you trust me not to burn you?" Amber asked.

Carmen's heart began to pound. Amber had put her trust in Carmen to keep her safe. Now she was faced with doing the same.

She nodded. "Yes, Mistress."

She lay still, her body tensed and waiting. Moments passed in silence, then seconds, then what felt like minutes.

Just as her guard began to slip, a drop of hot wax hit the skin below her shoulder. Reflexively, she squeezed her eyes shut tighter under the blindfold. At first, she could barely feel anything.

But after a moment, the heat surged to a peak. She inhaled sharply. Then, as slowly as the burning arose, it faded, leaving a faint tingling behind.

Again, Amber drizzled the hot wax onto Carmen's back, this time drawing a long, meandering line across it. Again, Carmen felt a sharply rising heat that set her skin ablaze, before dissipating through the rest of her body.

"Your skin looks so lovely, painted in red," Amber crooned. "Your body is the perfect canvas."

She dripped the wax onto Carmen's back again, painting it all over her skin, from her shoulders, down her back and ass cheeks, down the backs of her thighs. Carmen writhed against her bonds. Each drop of wax sizzled on her skin, already sensitized from the flogger's bite. And deep within her, desire roared.

But Amber wasn't done. She turned Carmen onto her back, the ropes at her wrists and ankles twisting, the hardened wax cracking on her skin. Then, she dribbled the wax over Carmen's front, up her thighs, up her stomach, until she reached her chest.

Carmen bit down on the inside of her cheek, burning with anticipation. With infuriating slowness, Amber dripped the wax over Carmen's breasts, her nipples, one after the other, sending darts of pleasure into her.

She shivered and moaned, her nipples forming stiff peaks under the cooling wax. Each drip, each fiery kiss on her skin, made her throb and ache between her thighs. She couldn't take any more of this. She was ready to combust.

Amber ran her hands up the front of Carmen's body, caressing her wax-speckled skin. Carmen strained toward her, desperate for more of her touch.

"That's it," Amber said. "Your Mistress is right here with you."

She leaned down, planting a brief kiss on Carmen's lips. Then, for a moment, there was only silence, as empty as the darkness surrounding her.

Carmen's head began to spin. Sightless, her hands bound, without Amber's touch to ground her, she was disoriented.

She made to call out Amber's name, then stopped herself. Instead, she drew in a breath, clearing the fog from her mind. If she concentrated, she could still make out

Amber's presence in the room, the scent of her perfume, the soft click of her heels on the floorboards. She was still safe in her Mistress's hands.

A moment later, Amber's footsteps approached the bed. Her feet were bare now, hardly making a sound. She stopped by the end of the bed and untied the ropes at Carmen's ankles, freeing them.

"You've managed to impress me tonight. I've had my doubts about whether you could truly let go of control, but here you are, laid out for me, my obedient pet." Amber drew a finger up the front of Carmen's leg. "It's time I rewarded you."

The bed began to sway, then Amber was at Carmen's knees, prying them apart. She settled between them, then swept her hand upward, up Carmen's stomach, up to her chest, up the mound of each breast and over each nipple, the wax cracking and crumbling under her fingertips.

Carmen quivered, her skin tender from the flogger and the heat of the wax, making the gentlest of touches feel heavenly.

Amber purred with satisfaction. "I'll never tire of hearing you come undone. It's every bit as sweet as I always imagined."

The throbbing in Carmen's center intensified. With Amber's body against hers, she could feel that her Mistress was naked now, not a scrap of lingerie between them. And something hard was pressing between her legs. A strap-on?

"I want to feel it," Amber whispered. "The moment when you unravel. I want you to come undone with me."

Carmen's heart began to race. She rarely found herself at

this end of a strap-on. But suddenly, she ached for Amber to fill her.

Amber slid the hard shaft down between Carmen's lower lips, skating it over her swollen clit and down to her entrance.

Slowly, she slipped it inside. Carmen drew in a halting gasp. As she relaxed into the sensation, Amber began moving inside her in careful, measured strokes, sending waves of pleasure through her. Her whole body trembled, an unrestrained moan falling from her.

"That's it," Amber said. "Come apart with me."

She buried herself deeper, rolling her hips against Carmen's. Blindfolded, her hands bound, Carmen could do little other than clutch at her Mistress's waist with her thighs. And soon, she realized that there were no straps around Amber's hips. The strap-on was strapless. So Amber could feel it too, could feel her inside, feel all the heights of bliss that Carmen felt with every thrust.

It was almost enough to tip her over the edge. But she fought against it, pulling herself back. She wanted to be with Amber like this for as long as she could. She wanted to make this moment stretch out to infinity.

She arched up, her legs clenching around Amber's hips, drawing her in. She relished the feel of Amber's silky skin on hers, of her lips on her neck and her breath on her skin, of the way her soft breasts moved against Carmen's as she surged against her.

And as they rocked together, the tide of Carmen's impending orgasm grew, until it became too strong to hold back. She tipped her head backward, rising into Amber, her entire body submerged in ecstasy.

But her cry was drowned out by that of her Mistress. Amber shuddered against her, pleasure washing through them both relentlessly. Together, they rode their climax like a storm as it stretched into that infinity Carmen had been seeking.

CHAPTER 17

Carmen lay in the bed, unbound now. Amber was stretched out next to her, her golden hair fanned out on the pillow beneath her head. Her skin glowed in the lamplight, illuminating the faint sprinkling of freckles across her shoulders and the small brown birthmark hiding at the base of one breast. It was almost shaped like an apple.

Seeing Amber like this, naked and spent, all of her laid bare, stirred something inside Carmen's chest. Did she find it as hard to be vulnerable with another person as Carmen did? She seemed so at ease, here and now.

And yet, so did Carmen.

Amber shifted onto her side, facing her. "You're looking pensive. What's on your mind?"

"Nothing," Carmen said. "I'm just thinking about how good this feels."

Amber smiled. "I like seeing you this way. Relaxed. Free." She stroked Carmen's arm with the backs of her fingers. "I saw something of that in you earlier today, with your sister. You're different when you're with her."

"The two of us are close, even for sisters. She was so young when we lost our parents, so now I'm all she has."

"You care about her a great deal, don't you?"

Carmen nodded. "I worry about her a lot too."

"That's only natural. She *is* a teenager, after all."

"You've got that right. She's a good kid, but she used to get in a lot of trouble, especially after our abuela died. She's doing better now, but still, I worry. She wants to move away for college, but I don't know if she's ready to be on her own. She sees me as overprotective, overbearing, but..." Carmen shook her head. "Maybe she's right. I just don't want to fail her again."

"Again?"

"It's complicated. My parents' deaths weren't an accident. They were killed. Jo and I were there."

A familiar mix of emotions surfaced in Carmen. Regret, sadness, longing, along with all those other feelings she'd never been able to pin down. But her guilt overshadowed them all.

"I'm sorry," Amber said. "I didn't mean to bring up something painful."

"It's okay. What happened to my parents has always been out in the open for me. It was all over the news at the time, so I never had the luxury of hiding from it. It was a home invasion. My parents were well known in the neighborhood because they owned a local business. The burglars targeted our house because they thought we had money there. They broke in one night with guns, but our mom heard them coming. Instead of calling for help, she used the time she had to hide me and my sister in the pantry and told us not to make a sound. Jo was only four, so I had to try hard to keep her quiet, but…"

Amber squeezed her arm gently. The sympathy in her eyes did little to quell Carmen's shame.

"But in the end, it wasn't her who couldn't stay silent," she said. "I was watching everything through the crack between the cupboard doors. While the burglars ransacked the house, one of them kept guard over my parents, a gun pointed at their heads. My mom kept pleading with him, but that just made him angry. So he hit her. Hard. And I screamed."

The events that followed were seared deep into Carmen's mind. It had taken years for her to stop reliving them every time she closed her eyes.

"The next thing I knew, the burglar made a move toward the pantry where we were hidden," she said. "What happened after that is a blur. My dad tried to stop him. There were gunshots, then my parents fell to the floor, one after the other. There was yelling, and then the pantry door opened. I think the burglars panicked at the sight of us, or just couldn't bring themselves to hurt children, so they fled. But even after they were gone, I stayed frozen in the pantry with my sister, watching our parents bleed to death. I didn't try to save them. I didn't call anyone. I didn't move until the police found us. I was too scared."

She fell silent, her gaze drifting toward the ceiling, avoiding Amber's eyes. She knew what was coming. The shock. The pity. The empty condolences. She hated it.

But Amber barely gave her the slightest sympathy. "I'm sorry your parents were taken from you like that," she said.

"But surely you don't blame yourself for what happened that night?"

"Who else is there to blame?" Carmen said. "If it wasn't for me, Jo would still have a mom and dad."

"You're not responsible for your parents' deaths. You were a child. What were you supposed to do?"

"I was 12. That's old enough. There are so many things I could have done, so many ways I could have stopped everything happening the way it did. But I was too scared. The fear I felt that night, I've never forgotten it. I've never forgotten how it paralyzed me." Something inside Carmen's chest tightened. "After that night, I decided I'd never let fear or weakness control me. After that night, I resolved to become strong so I could protect those around me, including my sister. But I'll never be able to make up for what happened."

"Look at me, Carmen."

Reluctantly, she obeyed.

"What did you tell me the other day when I was blaming myself for letting that stalker get to my mother?" Amber asked.

"I told you that you couldn't blame yourself for the actions of a crazy stalker. But that's completely different."

"How is it different? The burglars, they invaded your home with guns, intent on getting what they wanted with no regard for your family's lives. They're to blame for their actions. You didn't kill your parents. They did.

"I know I can't convince you to stop blaming yourself. But I know that your sister doesn't blame you for it, or for anything else. Jo looks up to you, admires you, thinks the world of you. I could tell just by watching the two of you together today. You haven't failed her. And I know you care about her too much to let that happen."

Carmen gave a non-committal murmur.

"You don't believe me, but it's true," Amber said. "I see you, Carmen. I see the way you put others first, caring for them, protecting them, sacrificing for them. You take on all this weight, this responsibility, and you carry it around with you, all because of the guilt you feel." She cupped Carmen's chin in her hand, looking deep into her eyes. "It's okay to let go of it, to allow yourself to be free."

Amber leaned in and kissed her gently. As Carmen sank into her lips, she tried to take the woman's words to heart.

But letting go of all her guilt was easier said than done.

CHAPTER 18

Amber greeted Gabrielle with a brief embrace. "Thank you for coming by."

"No problem," Gabrielle said, taking a seat next to her on the couch. "We all needed to get out of the office. The others are on their way."

It was early in the afternoon, and Amber, Gabrielle, and the other Mistress executives had a meeting scheduled. With Carmen insisting that she stay home as much as possible, Amber had planned to attend the meeting remotely like Lydia was, but Gabrielle had suggested everyone come to her instead.

"This gives us a chance to catch up, one on one," Gabrielle said. "With you under house arrest, it's been too long. Has there been any progress with this stalker issue?"

"Not yet," Amber replied. "But honestly, it's nothing to worry about. We're just being cautious."

"We?"

"Me and Carmen. My bodyguard. She thinks it's best to limit my movements. I'm simply following her advice."

Gabrielle raised an eyebrow. "Oh? A woman you actually listen to? I didn't think there was anyone in the world who could boss you around. This must be a new experience for you."

Amber ignored her friend's comment. "How are things with Dana and Chloe? I haven't heard from them in a while." Dana and Chloe were Gabrielle's girlfriends. How she managed with *two* girlfriends was beyond Amber.

"Things are great. Well, mostly. Chloe has moved in now, and our place is a madhouse. She brought her cat with her, and to say he's possessive is an understatement. He won't let either of us get a moment alone with her." Gabrielle threw her hands up. "I wasn't expecting to have to share our girl-friend with a territorial cat. But I suppose it's going to take some time for everyone to adjust."

Amber smiled. "Aren't you glad you listened to me when I told you to tell Chloe how you feel? No need to thank me for that. Although, I'll never understand how you find the time and energy for a relationship with *two* women."

Gabrielle's voice grew wistful. "That's the thing. When you love someone the way we do, being with each other is effortless, natural. They're a part of me. When I'm with them, I feel more at ease, like everything is exactly as it should be."

Amber couldn't deny how perfect the three of them were for each other. While many would consider their relation-ship unconventional, the three of them seemed to complete each other, fitting together like puzzle pieces.

What would it feel like to find that puzzle piece, that someone who fit her so perfectly? Amber had always thought that it was impossible, given what she wanted in a woman.

But perhaps she was wrong.

Her thoughts were interrupted by the arrival of Madison and Yvonne, Mistress Media's COO.

"Sorry we're late." Madison took a seat across from them. "We got carried away talking wedding business. Yvonne wanted the details of the vendors Blair and I used."

"Have you set a date, then?" Amber asked.

"Not yet," Yvonne replied. "We want to take our time to figure it all out. Given that our first wedding took place in a chapel in Vegas a few hours after we met, we want our real wedding to be perfect. And I want to give Ruby the fairy tale wedding of her dreams."

"I'm sure it will be incredible," Gabrielle said. "And speaking of your wedding, I talked to Dana, and she's happy to design your dresses."

"Wonderful. Ruby will be thrilled. She adores Dana's designs."

"Chloe wants to do your flowers, too. And you're having a bachelorette party, aren't you? Because those are my specialty. I'm going to throw one for you."

"That won't be necessary," Yvonne said firmly.

"But you *have* to have one. The only reason you met Ruby is because we were in Vegas for Madison's bachelorette party. And I'm the one who threw that party. So it's only fitting." Gabrielle's trademark mischievous smile grew on her face. "How about another weekend in Vegas? With Ruby, of course."

Yvonne threw her hands up in defeat. "All right. But only

if Ruby is on board. This whole wedding is for her, after all. I just want her to be happy."

"Aw, aren't you the doting wife?" Gabrielle said. "Er, fiancée? Either way, it's sweet."

Amber had to admit, it was sweet. Why was it that when she listened to all this talk of love and marriage, she found herself with a longing she couldn't ignore? Ever since she was young, she'd resisted the idea of settling down. It was, in part, a small rebellion against her mother, but it was also due to her own independent nature.

However, lately, she'd started to wonder if perhaps settling down wasn't such a bad idea. All her friends were married or in relationships, and their love-induced happiness was infectious.

As the conversation carried on around her, Amber noticed someone at the door to the room. She turned to find Carmen standing in the doorway, her arms crossed. She looked to have come from a session in the gym, her black workout leggings clinging to the toned muscles of her legs, her bare arms sheening with sweat.

Amber was so distracted by the sight that she almost missed the dark expression on Carmen's face. She knew that expression well, although the last time she'd seen it had been when they were in bed together at the summer residence, moments before Carmen had tried to storm out.

Carmen wasn't happy with her. What had she done?

Amber cleared her throat. "Will you excuse me for a moment?"

She rose from her seat and left the room, leading Carmen out into the hallway. "Is something the matter?"

Carmen's brows drew together. "Yes, something is the matter! What are you doing? Who are all these people?"

"You've already met Gabrielle. Madison and Yvonne work with me, too. Since you won't let me go into the office, they were kind enough to come to me so we could have a meeting."

"A meeting? You were talking about bachelorette parties!"

"We do get off topic sometimes."

Carmen shook her head. "It doesn't matter what they're doing here. We've already established that you need to clear any guests with me in advance. It's a potential security risk."

"My friends are hardly a threat to my security."

"Maybe not, but I need to know where you are and who you're with at all times. Any surprises, any variables, make it harder for me to protect you. I need to know what's going on."

"You're right." Amber tried her best to sound contrite. "I'm sorry. I promise that next time I have guests, I'll tell you in advance."

"That's all I'm asking."

Amber nodded. "While I have you here, I had your suit for the Pryce Foundation Ball sent to your room."

"My suit?"

"I had one made for you. As my personal bodyguard, you'll be with me the entire night, so you have to look like you belong. And you don't strike me as the type who wears dresses."

"I wear dresses sometimes," Carmen said. "They just aren't exactly practical for my job."

"Really? You, in a dress? I have to see this."

"Don't get your hopes up. It doesn't happen often."

"Oh, but I could make it happen. I *am* your Mistress, after all. You're mine to command." Amber looked around to ensure they were out of sight of prying eyes, then leaned in to speak in Carmen's ear. "Perhaps I should put you in a dress to make it easier to fuck the living daylights out of you."

A faint pink flush crept up Carmen's cheeks.

Amber smiled. "Or, perhaps I just like seeing that softer side of you." Teasing her, making her melt like this, was always so satisfying. The shimmer in her eyes, the way her lips would part, were a silent, irresistible challenge for Amber to kiss her.

But before she could, the butler strode by, carrying a tray of refreshments for everyone in the room beyond.

Amber took a reluctant step back. "I need to get back to it."

Carmen nodded. "I'll be in the gym if you need me."

Amber returned to the sitting room. As soon as she sat down, Gabrielle gave her a nudge.

"If you're going to be stuck at home, at least you have that bodyguard to keep you company," she said. "The two of you must be getting very cozy."

Gabrielle knew. It was written all over her face. Were the two of them that obvious?

But Gabrielle had known her since they were teenagers. She could read Amber better than anyone. And while everyone else in the room was looking at her curiously, they didn't say a word.

Before they had the chance to, Amber changed the

subject. "The Pryce Foundation Ball. It's this weekend. I take it you're all coming?"

"Of course," Madison said. "We wouldn't miss it. We know how hard you've been working on it."

In defiance of her mother, Amber had taken over planning the ball completely. She preferred to oversee everything herself, and she'd had to make several changes to her mother's plans in the name of security. Carmen had insisted on it.

And Amber hadn't fought her on the matter. With the stalker out there, lurking, getting bolder and bolder, she appreciated Carmen's extreme caution. Now, she found it reassuring rather than irritating.

As the conversation moved on to business, Amber thought back to Gabrielle's words. *When I'm with them, I feel more at ease.* Wasn't that how Carmen made her feel?

But was that because she was Amber's bodyguard, tasked with keeping her safe from this mysterious stalker?

Or was it something more?

CHAPTER 19

"Will you relax?" Amber hissed.

Carmen straightened her suit jacket as she scanned the ballroom. "I'm just trying to do my job."

It was the night of the Pryce Foundation Ball, and she and Amber were back at the place they'd first met that night at the charity auction. All these glitzy events were the same to her, but she knew how important this one was to Amber.

And the fact that the ball was in the Pryce family name meant that Amber's attendance was public knowledge. If there was a time or place for the stalker to strike, it was now. So Carmen had organized extra security, double the usual number for an event like this, and she'd made sure every single guest and member of staff had been thoroughly screened. No one was getting in uninvited.

But she wasn't taking any chances. And Amber had wanted to keep her nearby, despite her usual desire for her bodyguards to be invisible. Dressed in a suit, with her hair loose to cover her earpiece, Carmen passed as a guest well enough to blend in.

Amber let out an exasperated sigh. "I can't have you following me around looking like you're about to beat up anyone who approaches me. You'll scare everyone away."

Carmen took a step back. "Then I'll keep my distance."

"No, stay close. I want you at my side."

Carmen's stomach flickered. There was something in Amber's words, some hint of yearning beneath the coolness of her voice. Was she simply worried about the stalker making an appearance? Her desire to keep Carmen close almost felt like possessiveness.

Amber looked at her curiously. "Is everything all right?"

Carmen nodded.

"Are you sure? You're not going to tackle me again, are you? Because I really like this gown." The sleek red and gold evening gown Amber wore was just as expensive-looking as the dress she'd worn the night of the charity auction. And she looked just as breathtaking in it.

"Er, sorry about that. It won't happen again."

"I'm only joking. You really are wound tight tonight." Amber leaned close, letting her hand brush Carmen's. "If it makes it easier, we can pretend you're my date. You look the part, after all. Although, I would have liked to see you in a dress."

Warmth rose up Carmen's face. "Like I told you, that wouldn't be very practical."

"I'm not complaining. That suit looks as striking on you as I imagined. If we weren't surrounded by people, I'd make a point of finding out how quickly I could tear it off you." Amber drew back. "But we don't have time for that tonight. I have so much work to do."

"Work? You mean making small talk with all these people?"

"That *is* work. All of this is about making connections, and using those connections to do some good. Each and every person in this room was handpicked to be here for that exact purpose." She looked around the hall, her eyes zeroing in on a nearby couple. "You see Councilwoman Reid over there? She's a bleeding heart when it comes to a good cause. Her girlfriend, on the other hand, isn't the charitable type, but she comes from money and has lots of it. Together, they're perfect candidates to become regular donors for the Pryce Foundation. That's why I invited them here tonight. And I'm making sure to give them extra attention."

Carmen shook her head. "I don't understand any of this."

"It's just business. Come on, let's go talk to the councilwoman."

The rest of the hour was spent talking not only to the councilwoman, but to dozens of other people with equally important titles. Following Amber around while she made polite conversation with everyone was even duller than keeping an eye on her from afar.

But as time wore on, Carmen found herself relaxing a little. The night was half over and there hadn't been a single incident, aside from a pair of drunk guests almost getting into a fight. But Carmen's team had put a stop to that before anything could happen. With the amount of security at the event, no one was getting to Amber.

As they took a moment to breathe between conversations, Amber summoned a nearby server, plucking a glass of champagne from his tray. He then presented the tray to Carmen, offering her a drink.

"One little glass couldn't hurt," Amber said.

Carmen shook her head, dismissing him. "I'm working. Drinking on the job would be unprofessional."

"I could fire you. Just for tonight. I'll hire you again in the morning."

Carmen shook her head, but she couldn't hold off the smile pulling at her lips.

"Now this is the Carmen I like to see. The real Carmen." Amber gazed back at her, her eyes alight. "I wasn't joking about having you here as my date. We could drink all the champagne we wanted, dance the night away. It would be thrilling, wouldn't it? And it would give all these guests something to talk about. Amber Pryce having a secret affair with her bodyguard?"

That much was true. The crowd at the ball seemed like the kind that would find something like that scandalous.

"Wouldn't it be nice if we could do that?" Amber said. "Just forget about everything, throw caution to the wind, and be together?"

Carmen studied her face. There was a wistfulness in her voice, in her expression, that made Carmen's heart race.

"I…" Suddenly, she noticed something out of the corner of her eye, a familiar woman staring at them intently.

Aware of how close she and Amber were standing, she took a step back.

Amber followed the direction of her gaze and let out an irritated sigh. "That would be Gabrielle. I should go talk to her, she said she needed to speak to me."

Carmen followed Amber across the room to where

Gabrielle stood with a pair of other women, one tall and willowy with deep brown skin, the other shorter with strawberry blonde curls.

"You wanted to talk?" Amber said.

"Good evening to you too." Gabrielle glanced in Carmen's direction. "Aren't you going to introduce us?"

"She's my bodyguard. You've already met."

"Not properly," Gabrielle said.

"All right. Carmen, this is Gabrielle, Mistress Media's CMO and a good friend from childhood. This is Dana, and Chloe. They're her girlfriends."

Carmen gave them all a silent nod. Why was Gabrielle looking at her with such probing eyes?

"Nice to finally meet you," Gabrielle said. "I'm glad Amber has someone like you looking out for her. I imagine you two are spending lots of time together. All those long days, locked up in that house. And those long nights."

What? Carmen glanced at Amber. Had she told Gabrielle about the two of them?

But Amber's face gave nothing away. "What was it that you wanted, Gabi?" she asked coldly.

"I need to ask you something." She gave Dana and Chloe an apologetic look. "Secret Mistress business, I'm afraid. It won't take long."

"That's all right," Dana said. "We need to talk to Yvonne and Ruby about their wedding plans." She took Chloe's hand. "Come, let's go find them."

Amber turned to Carmen. "Excuse us for a moment."

Carmen stepped to the side, just out of earshot, and stood by, waiting. A minute passed, then another.

She glanced around at the crowd surrounding her. She'd

worked events like this plenty of times. Fancy parties, balls and fundraisers. But she'd never been in the thick of it like this. It felt different from the other side.

As she turned back to where Amber and Gabrielle stood, her stomach dropped.

Amber was gone.

She marched over to Gabrielle. "Where is she? Amber, where did she go?"

The woman shrugged. "I don't know. We finished talking and she walked off."

Carmen looked around frantically. But the crowd was too thick. She couldn't see Amber anywhere.

"I'm sure she's fine," Gabrielle said. "She's probably just talking to someone else."

But Carmen barely heard her. Amber wouldn't just walk off like that. Did something happen?

Did someone take her?

She cursed to herself. She let her guard down for a second, and Amber was gone.

But she didn't have time to beat herself up. She pushed through the crowd, seeking out a better vantage point. As she tapped her earpiece to contact the rest of her team, she caught a flash of a familiar red dress—*Amber's dress*—as the woman slipped through a door at the side of the hall.

Edging past a server carrying a tray of drinks, she made a beeline for the door. It opened to a flight of stairs that led to the balconies overlooking the ballroom.

She climbed the stairs. The hallway at the top of them was dark and deserted, the balconies closed to the public for the event. This was *not* good. If something happened to

Amber up here, if the stalker had lured her into the darkness, no one would see a thing.

Carmen reached into her jacket, her hand on the gun she had holstered inside it. She always carried it with her when on the job, but she rarely touched it. It was a last resort only.

And she prayed she wouldn't need to use it.

She edged down the hall, taking care to keep her footsteps silent. One by one, she searched each of the balcony rooms. But there were no signs of Amber, or anyone else. And other than the music playing in the ballroom downstairs, she couldn't hear a sound.

She reached the final balcony. Taking a deep breath, she peered into it. In the dim light, she could make out a figure standing by the balustrade, looking down at the hall below.

It was Amber. And she was alone.

She felt a surge of relief. "Amber?"

As Carmen stepped into the room, Amber turned to her. And on her face was a single tear.

CHAPTER 20

A mber turned her back to the doorway, wiping her eyes. Carmen seeing her in a rare moment of weakness was not what she needed right now.

But Carmen didn't say a word, instead joining Amber by the balustrade, silently.

"I know," Amber said. "I shouldn't have gone off alone. I hope I didn't worry you."

"Well, for a moment, I was convinced you'd been abducted and dragged up here by the stalker," Carmen said. "But I'm glad you're all right."

That hadn't occurred to Amber at all. "I'm sorry, I just needed a moment to myself."

"Are you okay?"

"Tonight just has me feeling sentimental." All it had taken was an idle comment from Gabrielle about how wonderful the ball was this year, and every emotion she'd been holding back the entire night rose to the surface. "Being here, as the only Pryce, is bittersweet. This ball, it's been a family tradition since before I was born. I've always

169

loved them. At least I used to, until the year that I ruined everything."

"What do you mean?"

"It was two years ago. The ball had taken place during a difficult time for me and my family. In the space of a few months, my father had passed away, and my mother had gotten sick. There was a chance she wouldn't make it, and I thought I was going to lose her, too. I was going to be alone.

"I'm ashamed to admit it, but it all became too much for me. I couldn't hold myself together any longer, couldn't keep being the perfect daughter everyone needed me to be. I went off the rails entirely, drowning myself in alcohol and every other vice I could find, all to numb the pain I felt. That went on for months. And then the Pryce Foundation Ball came along."

"What happened?" Carmen asked.

"I turned up drunk. I made a fool of myself, made a scene, had a big public fight with my mother. She'd just gotten out of the hospital, mind you, and was still dealing with the aftermath of my father's death. I said such awful things to her, and in front of everyone."

Amber gripped the balcony railing tightly. "It was enough to snap me back to reality. After that night, I sobered up and dug myself out of the hole I'd crawled into. But I've never forgotten that night, the way I cracked under the pressure. And I'm never going to live it down."

Carmen slid her hand across the railing, touching it to Amber's. "I'm sure no one holds your actions that night against you. You were going through a difficult time. You were grieving. You're only human."

"Perhaps. But I don't get to be human. I don't get to

make mistakes. I need to be perfect. That's what everyone expects of me. And my mother has never let me forget it. Being here tonight is a reminder that I'll never live up to all this, to her legacy. She'll always see me as inadequate." Yet, at the same time, Amber wished she were here.

"Are you sure she feels that way? I don't know your mother, but I don't see how any parent could look at you and not be proud of the woman you are."

"If she is, she's never said it. She's disappointed in me, I know it. She has this idea of who she wants me to be, what kind of life she wants for me, but it's not the life that I want. She'll never be happy with the choices I make. I just wish she would be proud of me as I am."

"Have you ever told her this?"

"Not in as many words. Every time the topic comes up, we end up fighting. It makes me feel so guilty, creating this tension between us, given her condition. Every time I see her, I worry that it will be the last time. I just wish I could find a way to let her know how I feel."

"I'm sure she'd want to know how you feel. And I'm sure she's proud of you, even if she doesn't tell you that." Carmen hesitated. "My dad, he never used to say things like that to me. He never said *I love you*, even though, looking back, he showed it in other ways. But I never noticed that when I was a kid. So one day, I asked him if he loved me."

Amber glanced sideways at Carmen. Her face turned toward the ballroom beyond, but Amber could still make out the emotion in the bodyguard's eyes.

Her voice quavered as she spoke. "He was so shocked that I'd even need to ask him that question. He said, *Of course I love you*. He said he loved me more than words could express, which was why he'd never tried to express it. But that day, he said those words to me. And that conversation was one of the last I ever had with him."

She turned to Amber. "If you don't tell your mom how you feel while you have the chance, you'll regret it for the rest of your life."

"You're right," Amber said quietly.

"Then talk to her."

"I will. I'll talk to her." She gave Carmen a soft smile. "Just as soon as I'm permitted to see her again. I have this stickler of a bodyguard who has me under lock and key."

"We can make an exception, just this once."

Amber nodded. "Thank you. You've been such a help to me. Not just tonight. These past weeks, months, have been harder than I like to admit. I don't know if I could have gotten through them without you by my side."

"I'm glad I could be here for you."

Silence fell over them. Together, they looked down over the ballroom, watching the guests dance and mingle as the music played on.

Amber turned to Carmen. "It's beautiful, isn't it?"

Carmen nodded in agreement. Up here, the only light that reached them came from the chandelier hanging over the ballroom. And in the low light, Carmen's face seemed softer, less hardened by the harsh world that had inflicted so much pain and loss on her. What Amber would give to hold her in her arms, to kiss her, until all her hurts were healed.

She slid her hand up Carmen's arm. Carmen turned to her, dark eyes filled with passion. Something stirred inside Amber then, an insatiable need for the woman before her.

Drawing Carmen into her arms, she pulled her to the darkest corner of the balcony, out of view of any curious eyes from the ballroom below, and pressed her lips to Carmen's. The kiss was tender but unyielding, desperate but demanding. Carmen melted against her, the heat of her body setting Amber alight. Their need for one another combined into a raging inferno, feeding off their shared desire.

Their lips still locked, Amber slid Carmen's jacket from her shoulders, letting it fall to the floor. She ran her hands down Carmen's front, feeling the curves of her chest, her waist, her hips, relishing the firmness of her toned stomach. Carmen quivered under her fingers, murmured into her lips, arched into her touch, her body surrendering.

Something surged inside Amber, a primal hunger. "I need you," she growled.

She reached down between them and unbuttoned Carmen's pants, slipping her hand inside her panties. Carmen parted her legs, yielding to her reflexively. Amber skated a fingertip over Carmen's clit, then slid her hand down to her entrance, making her body shiver and ripple against her.

"Yes," Carmen said, breathless. "*Please.*"

Amber exhaled sharply. Seeing—feeling—Carmen like this, so pliant and needy, slowly coming undone, only made Amber want to take her apart altogether.

Pushing Carmen against the wall beside them, she slipped her fingers into her. Carmen drew in a gasp, her whole body shuddering. Amber worked her fingers, stroking and delving, reveling in Carmen's slickness, her heat, the way she would throb and pulse when Amber nudged that sweet spot inside. She ground her hips in time, her chest hitching, and grasped at Amber's shoulders and the sides of her neck, holding on tightly, not allowing anything but the faintest of murmurs to escape her.

And as those murmurs rose and rose, the need aching deep within Amber intensified, spurred on by the sweet sounds Carmen made. She was close. Amber could feel it. A part of her wanted to pull back, to keep Carmen suspended in this state of bliss for as long as she could, savoring every pleading moan, feeling her buck and tremble without restraint.

But the rest of her wanted to send Carmen's pleasure skyrocketing to such great heights that she would lose herself entirely.

So she let their fevered thrusts escalate until they reached a crescendo. Carmen's grip on Amber's shoulders tightened, her head tipping back against the wall as an orgasm seized her. She convulsed and quaked, clinging to Amber as if trying to keep from drowning in endless ecstasy.

And when her climax passed, and she came up for air, Amber pulled her into a greedy, urgent kiss. While Carmen might have been satisfied, the hunger in Amber had only grown. She needed Carmen to sate it.

But before she could issue a single command, Carmen broke the kiss. She drew back.

She looked deep into Amber's eyes.

Then, she dropped to her knees.

The fire inside Amber raged. How far the two of them had come. Carmen didn't need to be told what Amber needed from her anymore. She knew it intuitively. And she was giving it enthusiastically, without the slightest hesitation.

Wordlessly, she reached underneath Amber's dress and slid her hands up Amber's legs, over her hips and up to her panties. Then, she looked up at Amber and waited, a silent question in her eyes.

Amber answered her in kind, drawing her dress up further, holding it around her hips. Carmen took the waistband of Amber's panties and slid them down to the ground. Amber stepped out of them, one heeled foot after another, then parted her legs.

Still on her knees, Carmen dipped down, her lips brushing the top of Amber's foot. She kissed her way up Amber's ankle, up the inside of her calf and her knee. She kissed her way up Amber's thigh, her full, soft lips tickling Amber's skin. She kissed her way up, until finally, she reached the peak where Amber's thighs met.

Amber quivered, falling back against the wall behind her. "Yes. Worship me."

Parting Amber's lower lips with her tongue, Carmen slipped it between them and ran it up and down. Amber let out a hard breath, pleasure darting through her.

Carmen drew her mouth up to Amber's clit, pursing her lips around it, sucking and teasing, strumming with her tongue. Amber spread her legs wider, pushing her hips out. As she lost herself in increasing ecstasy, she released her hold on her dress, letting it fall over Carmen's head. Still, Carmen continued, working between Amber's thighs with reverent fervor, until finally, she tipped over the edge.

Her mouth fell open in a silent moan as a wave of pleasure engulfed her. She trembled uncontrollably, her thighs clenching. One hand sprawled on the wall behind her, she grasped at Carmen through her dress, clutching tightly onto the other woman as she rode out the unrelenting climax.

When her orgasm finally subsided, and Carmen had disentangled herself from underneath her dress, Amber reached down and cradled her face in her hands, drawing her to her feet. They crashed together in a kiss so all-consuming that Amber lost any sense of where her body ended and Carmen's began.

Suddenly, Carmen's earpiece began to crackle and hiss.

Carmen groaned. Amber pried herself away, reality returning. They'd been up here for some time now. Had their absence been noticed?

Carmen put her finger on her earpiece. "Wheeler? What's going on?" She paused, turning away. "I'm with her now. We're upstairs, having a breather. Is something wrong?"

Amber frowned. Carmen's voice was becoming increasingly more concerned.

"We're on our way," Carmen finally said. "We'll meet you at the bottom of the stairs."

Carmen turned back to her.

"Is everything all right?" Amber asked.

"There's some kind of situation. I need to talk to Wheeler. Let's go."

Amber raised an eyebrow. "We're not going anywhere looking like this."

Carmen glanced down at her clothes. "Right."

She picked up Amber's panties and handed them to her, then straightened out her own clothes and slipped her jacket back on. Producing a compact from her purse, Amber fixed her hair and lipstick before giving Carmen a nod.

They left the room and headed down the stairs. Waiting for them at the bottom were Wheeler and Hudson.

Hudson stared at them both, his brows drawn together. Was he onto them?

But Amber didn't have time to deal with that now. "Well? Are you going to tell us what's going on?"

Wheeler cleared his throat. "There's been a minor incident. But you're not in any danger. Everything has been taken care of."

"Enough beating around the bush. Just tell me what happened."

"Someone was caught lurking around the perimeter of the building. When my guys tried to approach her, she ran away. They gave chase, but she escaped."

Carmen cursed. "Did anyone get a look at her face?"

Hudson nodded. "I saw her, but it was too dark to make out her features clearly. From what I could see, she fit the description. White female, average height, long black hair. She was dressed for a party, too. She was obviously trying to get in."

Amber turned to Carmen. "That sounds like her."

"It's likely," Wheeler said. "We're checking the security cameras to see if they caught anything. Maybe we'll luck out and get some footage that shows her face clearly."

Carmen nodded. "In the meantime, tell everyone to keep their eyes open in case she shows up again. There's only another hour or so before the ball ends, so make sure everyone is on high alert for the rest of the night. Let's get back to work."

"Wait." Amber turned to Hudson. "The woman. What was she wearing?"

Hudson shrugged. "A dress? A black one, I think."

"Did she have any jewelry on?"

"Now that you mention it, she was wearing a necklace. This big, black choker thing. Didn't seem to match the rest of the outfit."

Amber gave him a nod. "You're dismissed."

As soon as the men were out of sight, she exchanged a glance with Carmen, neither of them saying a word. They'd both come to the same conclusion.

The collar. The woman was definitely the stalker.

But why was she always wearing it? And what did it mean?

CHAPTER 21

Amber strode through her wing at the Pryce residence in search of Carmen. She wanted to find out whether her team had made any progress in finding footage of the stalker from the ball. It had been a few days since that night, and they hadn't uncovered anything yet.

But Carmen wasn't anywhere in the wing. There was only one other place she was likely to be.

And that was exactly where Amber found her, in the mansion's gym. Carmen didn't usually work out in the mornings. Was she feeling on edge? Amber herself had been feeling tense ever since the ball.

She stopped in the doorway, watching Carmen. The gym was outfitted with the best equipment money could buy, yet here Carmen was, doing push-ups on the bare floor, headphones in her ears. She was dressed in a sports bra and workout leggings, the sleek muscles of her arms and back glistening with sweat.

Was this tough Marine really the same woman who had

dropped to her knees before Amber on that dark balcony the other night?

After a final dozen push-ups, Carmen sprung to her feet. Only then did she notice Amber standing in the doorway.

She pulled her earbuds out of her ears. "You scared me. How long have you been there?"

Amber stepped into the room. "Long enough. Don't stop for me. I was enjoying the show."

"I've finished anyway." Carmen grabbed her towel from a nearby chair, wiping the sweat from her flushed face before hanging it around her neck. "Was there something you wanted?"

"Perhaps I simply wanted to watch you. Is that a crime?" She folded her arms across her chest. "But you're right, I do want something. I came to ask if you have any updates on the situation with the stalker."

Carmen shook her head. "The team is still looking at the footage from the other night, but it'll take a while to get through it all. Sorry I don't have anything more for you."

"Don't be sorry. You've done more than enough for me. And I'm ever grateful to have a knight in shining armor to protect me, and such a strong one at that." Amber stepped closer to her and drew a hand up her muscled arm. "But I do appreciate that my knight has a softer side too."

Carmen's face, already flushed from her workout, turned even redder. Amber felt a pang of satisfaction. It was delightful, the way Carmen turned into a quivering mess whenever Amber touched her.

"So what were you doing in here so early?" she asked.

"Just blowing off some steam," Carmen replied.

"I understand. All this stress has me feeling the need to let off some steam, too. I could use a workout too."

"Oh? What did you have in mind?"

Amber took the ends of the towel around Carmen's neck, pulling her in close. "I believe what you meant to say is, 'What did you have in mind, Mistress Amber?'"

Carmen let out a hard breath that had nothing to do with exertion. But before either of them could speak, Amber heard the shuffle of footsteps out in the hallway.

She dropped the towel, turning to see one of the guards, Hudson, appear at the door.

Carmen pulled away abruptly. Hudson cleared his throat and gave her a nod.

"Excuse me for a minute," she said.

She walked over to Hudson, exchanging some words with him. Then he left the room, but not before giving Amber a suspicious glance. He'd obviously figured out that there was something between Carmen and Amber. With everything that was going on, Amber was beyond caring, but she suspected that Carmen wasn't as indifferent.

However, she didn't have a chance to broach the topic before Carmen spoke. "That was a message from Wheeler. We have our stalker on video. And we have a clear look at her face."

A combination of apprehension and relief overcame Amber. "I need to see this footage."

"I'll go talk to Wheeler. Meet you in the living room."

They left the gym, Amber heading to the living room. She was finally going to see the face of whoever it was who had been dogging her for months now. She would finally get to the bottom of this mystery.

Ten minutes later, Carmen appeared holding a laptop, Wheeler at her side. She set the laptop before Amber and opened it up. The screen showed a video, paused, of a tall fence and a sidewalk beside it.

"This is from one of the side cameras outside the building," Carmen said. "We got a ton of footage of the woman lurking around for almost half an hour before she got spotted. Most of it is useless, but we got lucky with this."

Carmen pressed play, then fast-forwarded the video. On screen, the sidewalk was deserted. But after a few seconds, a woman in a black dress appeared, crossing the screen several times while walking back and forth past the fence for several minutes.

Finally, the woman stopped at the fence, turning fully toward the camera. Then, spotting it, she hurried down the street, out of view of the camera.

Carmen rewound the video and paused it on the frame that showed the woman's face clearest. "There. We have her."

Amber examined her. She fit the description they had of the stalker. And she was wearing the leather collar, just like Hudson had said.

Carmen spoke up beside her. "So, do you recognize her?"

"No," Amber replied. "I've never seen her before."

But even as the words left her mouth, she felt a sense of familiarity and dread. Did she know the woman in the collar somehow?

She shook her head. "I'm sorry, but I have no idea who she is. She isn't anyone I know."

Carmen cursed. "I was hoping you'd be able to ID her. Still, this gives us something to work with."

"That's right," Wheeler said. "I have some contacts in the police department. I've pulled some strings, and they're running the picture through their facial recognition databases. If she has a record, if she's ever been arrested anywhere in the country, she'll be in a database. It's a long shot, but it's more than we had a day ago."

Amber nodded. "As soon as you find anything, let me know."

"Yes, Ma'am." He took the laptop and closed the lid.

As soon as he was out of the room, Carmen put her hand on Amber's.

"Are you all right?" she asked.

Amber nodded. "I'm fine."

"Are you sure? You look pale."

"It's a little unnerving, that's all. Seeing the face of the woman who has made my life hell these past months..." That was what had Amber feeling so unsettled, wasn't it?

"I know." Carmen gave Amber's hand a sympathetic squeeze. "And you're sure you don't recognize her?"

"I'm sure." So why did she feel like she knew the woman somehow? She couldn't remember ever meeting her.

And along with that sense of familiarity, that dread, Amber felt something else.

Guilt.

Later that night, after a quick phone call to check up on her sister, Carmen left her room to find Amber. She was worried about her. Something about seeing the woman's face had rattled Amber deeply.

Carmen found her in the parlor where she'd left her, reclining in a loveseat with her phone in her hand. But she wasn't looking at it. Instead, she was gazing absently out the window.

Carmen entered the room, prompting Amber to snap out of her trance.

She gave Carmen a small smile. "How's your sister doing?"

"She's fine," Carmen replied. "She says hi. Ever since she met you, she's been a little obsessed with you."

"I hate to disappoint her, but I only have eyes for one Torres sister." She took Carmen's hand and pulled her down to sit next to her. "I just made a phone call of my own, to my mother. I'm taking your advice. I'm going to talk to her about everything. She'll be in town for a doctor's appointment next week, so we arranged to meet up for dinner afterward. That is, if you're okay with it. She doesn't like coming to the house anymore, not since my father passed."

Carmen nodded. "As long as you clear the location with me so I can make sure it's secure."

"I'll keep that in mind."

"How are you doing otherwise?" Carmen asked.

"I'm fine." Amber hesitated. "Seeing the woman's face makes everything seem much more real, that's all. And she's just not giving up. Who knows what she'll do next?"

"I know. But whatever happens, I'm not going to let her get to you. We'll figure this out."

Amber's only response was a non-committal murmur. Carmen had never seen her act like this—unsettled, uncertain, unsure. Why did Carmen get the feeling that there was something more going on, something that Amber wasn't letting on about?

But perhaps this was just Amber being Amber. She wasn't used to being vulnerable. And with the threat of the stalker hanging over her like a dark cloud, she was probably feeling more vulnerable than ever. Shutting down, shutting everyone out, was a natural reaction for her.

That had to be it. Carmen's suspicions were just in her head. After all, when it came to Amber, she found it hard to think rationally.

Her phone buzzed in her pocket, interrupting her thoughts. Given that it was after hours, it was either her sister or someone on her team contacting her about something important. "Let me check this quickly."

It was a text from Wheeler. *Come see me in the office ASAP.*

"Is something wrong?" Amber asked.

"Wheeler wants me," Carmen replied. "I'll be right back."

She got up and left Amber's wing. The urgency of the message was concerning. Had Wheeler found a match for the woman in the facial recognition database?

Then why did he only want to see Carmen, and not Amber too?

She headed to the office near the front of the house where the security team had set up shop. Wheeler was sitting at a desk inside. She announced herself before entering the room.

"Torres," he said. "Have a seat."

Carmen sat down tentatively. "Did you find a match?"

"Yes, but I need to speak to you about something first."

He shifted uncomfortably. "There are rumors going around the team. About you and the client. Ms. Pryce."

Carmen cursed internally. While they'd been careful to keep everything between them behind closed doors, apparently they hadn't been careful enough.

But before she could come up with any kind of excuse, Wheeler held up his hands. "If there's something going on there, I do not want to know. I get it. Tensions are high, people are working in close proximity. It's the perfect storm. These things happen. But you can't let them compromise your judgment. You have a job to do. You need to be able to do it."

Carmen nodded. "I know that. I won't let anything get in the way of my job."

"And if that changes, you need to let me know and I'll take you off this contract and find you something else, no questions asked."

"That won't be necessary. I can keep my head." But hadn't Carmen just been thinking that she found it hard to think rationally when it came to Amber?

"Good, because you're the most level-headed team member I have. I can't afford to lose you. So keep it together." Clearly relieved to have the conversation out of the way, Wheeler grabbed a file from his desk. "I got the results of the database search back. We got a hit. See for yourself."

Carmen took the file from him and opened it up. The first page was a rap sheet, complete with a mug shot. The woman in the picture had blonde hair, but her black roots were visible beneath, and her face matched that of the woman they'd caught on video. Her name was Michelle Glover, and she was 30 years old.

And Amber really didn't know who Michelle was? She'd said as much. But there had been a hesitance in her voice when she'd denied knowing the woman.

Carmen scanned the rest of the page, taking all the information in. Michelle had been arrested twice. The first arrest was over a fight at a bar which had led to a minor assault charge, but no jail time.

However, the second was far from minor. Michelle had been charged with assault with a deadly weapon and sentenced to five years in prison, having been released only a few years ago. According to a more detailed report on the next page, after Michelle's girlfriend broke up with her, she'd gotten violent and had threatened her with a knife.

Carmen cursed. They were dealing with someone dangerous.

"As you can see, Glover is a serious threat," Wheeler said. "I'll get in touch with the police in the morning and take what evidence we have to them."

Carmen nodded. "I'll let Amber know what's going on. Mind if I take this?"

"Sure. I figured you should be the one to tell her since you two are… close."

She grimaced. What exactly were the rumors that were going around? And who knew the truth? At the very least, Hudson had figured it out, judging by the looks that he kept giving them. And nothing stayed secret on a team as tight-knit as theirs.

She left the office and headed back to the parlor. As soon as she walked through the door, Amber was on her feet.

"What's the matter?" she asked. "Has something happened?"

"The stalker," Carmen said. "We've found out who she is."

She told Amber all about Michelle before handing her the file to see for herself. As Amber examined the mug shot, her face froze in an inscrutable mask. But there was something in her eyes, something like recognition.

"So you really don't know her?" Carmen asked. "Nothing here jogs your memory?"

Amber shook her head. "Nothing. I've never met this woman in my life."

Carmen held back a frown. Amber was being far too calm about this. Her demeanor felt forced. Was it just shock?

She put the file down. "I'm having trouble processing this. It's disconcerting to know that someone this dangerous is after me. Where has this obsession she has with me even come from?"

"Speculation isn't going to help us. Michelle's motivations don't matter. What matters is that we're going to get to the bottom of this. The police are looking into the matter now. And until we have this worked out, I'm going to make sure to keep you out of harm's way."

Amber nodded. "And I appreciate it. But for now, I need a moment to myself. Do you mind?"

"Sure. Let me know if you need me."

As Carmen got up to leave, Amber picked up the file again, studying it with narrowed eyes.

What did she know?

CHAPTER 22

A few days later, as Carmen performed her evening check of the outer perimeter of the Pryce residence, Wheeler approached her.

"Do you have a moment?" he asked. "I need to speak with you."

She nodded. "Sure."

As she followed him into the house, she could feel the tension radiating from him, along with everyone else they passed. It was almost like it was coming from the house itself. Ever since they'd learned the identity of Amber's stalker, learned how dangerous she was, everyone was on high alert.

And now that they had a positive ID on her, the police were finally taking action. With all the letters and pictures Michelle had sent, there was enough evidence to charge her, or at least get a restraining order. The police were searching for her, but they hadn't been able to locate her yet.

Michelle was still out there, somewhere. So Carmen had barely left Amber's side. She was on edge, and so was

Amber. She was trying to hide it, but Carmen could tell. She knew Amber so intimately now that she could see it, clear as day. But every time Carmen tried to speak to her about how she felt, Amber would brush her off.

They reached the security team's office at the front of the house. Once inside, Wheeler shut the door before taking a seat at his desk.

"What's going on?" Carmen asked.

Wheeler opened a drawer and pulled out an envelope. "The stalker sent another letter to the house."

"What does it say?" For the sake of safety, Amber had left the task of opening her mail to the security team. With the stalker becoming increasingly brazen, there was a chance she'd send something that would put Amber at harm. They couldn't take that risk.

"It contains... sensitive content," he said. "I thought you should be the one to show it to Amber."

Carmen frowned. What the hell was in that letter?

"I don't know if any of it's true," Wheeler said. "It's probably just the ramblings of a delusional woman. Either way, it confirms how obsessed she is. She's dangerous."

Carmen took the letter from him. "I'll get this to her right away."

She left the room, letter in hand. But as she approached Amber's wing, she slowed her pace. What did the letter say? Perhaps it was best for Carmen to read it first so that she wouldn't be blindsided.

Her curiosity getting the best of her, she opened up the envelope. Inside was a photograph, along with a letter.

Carmen looked at the photo first. It was a selfie of the woman, Michelle, wearing a strapless dress and the same leather collar she always wore. But her hair was blonde like in her mug shot, not black. When had the photo been taken?

She looked at the background of the photo. It showed a spacious bedroom, like something from an expensive hotel, with elaborate wallpaper and a large bed in the middle. Beside the bed was a table holding an array of alcoholic drinks and several glasses. Strewn on top of the rumpled bedding lay an assortment of kinky sex toys. Handcuffs. Ropes. Several different kinds of whips.

Carmen frowned. *What is this?* She flipped the photo over. Scrawled on the back in the stalker's handwriting were three words.

Do you remember?

She slipped the photo back into the envelope and withdrew the letter. It was almost a dozen pages long, longer than anything the stalker had ever sent. And it began with the very same words that were written on the back of the photograph.

Do you remember the night we spent together? I do. I dream about it every time I close my eyes. I've never forgotten it. I've never forgotten you. I still wear your collar. I'm still yours.

Carmen's stomach swirled. These words were nothing more than the ramblings of someone with an imagined relationship with Amber.

But as she read on, the unease in her stomach grew. The letter described, in explicit detail, an intimate encounter with Amber. It described how the letter writer—Michelle— had met Amber at an exclusive club, a place where people went to indulge their darkest desires. How the two of them had shared a few drinks before Amber had taken the woman back to a hotel room. How the two of them had engaged in a long night of erotic games.

I remember the way the ropes felt as you bound me to the chair... the crack of the whip against my skin... your collar around my neck, your touch in the tenderest of places...

Carmen's heart sank. This felt too real, too personal. Was everything in the letter true? How would Michelle know about Amber's tastes in bed otherwise?

She shook her head. Surely this was just a fantasy formed by Michelle's obsessed mind. Carmen needed to stop now, to give Amber the letter.

But instead, she read on.

I remember it all. But most of all, I remember how, afterward, I spent hours worshiping your body, tracing every inch of your skin with my fingers... those freckles on your shoulders, that apple-shaped birthmark underneath your breast...

Suddenly, the air left Carmen's chest. Amber's birthmark. There was no way the woman could have known about that. Not unless she had seen it.

Everything in the letter was true. Was that why Amber had been acting so evasive? Because she knew who Michelle was and she'd lied about it?

Carmen swallowed, forcing herself to finish the letter. There was only one page left. And on it was a single sentence, one that seemed as much a threat as a wish.

I want to go back to that night, that room, and relive it with you, over and over.

The letter ended there, unsigned.

Carmen took out the photo and looked at it again. It had to have been taken that night.

Do you remember?

Amber paced her sitting room, unable to stay still. The anxiety and guilt she'd felt upon finding out the identity of her stalker had grown and grown until it had consumed her completely. She couldn't stop thinking about the stalker, the woman with the collar. And when she closed her eyes, all she could see was the woman's face.

And she could feel the walls closing in around her, could feel the pressure. It only made her more uneasy. The last time she'd felt this way, two years ago, she'd cracked under the strain. She couldn't let that happen again.

Behind her, someone cleared their throat.

Amber spun around to see Carmen standing in the doorway. She'd been so distracted that she hadn't noticed her. Her bodyguard's expression was even harder than usual.

"Is something the matter?" Amber asked.

Carmen held something out to her. An envelope. The handwriting on it was instantly recognizable.

Amber's heart began to pound. "What does it say?"

"See for yourself," Carmen replied.

Amber took the envelope and opened it up to find a letter inside, along with a photo of Michelle. As she examined it, that sense of familiarity and dread grew.

Pushing it down, she placed the photo on a table beside her and began reading the letter. With every line, the gnawing in her stomach intensified. The things the letter said, the details, they were all so graphic, so intimate. Amber had been right when she'd wondered if the stalker was aware of her sexual tastes, which she didn't reveal to anyone outside of her close personal circle.

But midway through the letter, all the pieces fell into place. The club. Michelle. The drinks, the hotel room, even more drinks. She only remembered parts of it. And those parts were hazy, like a bad dream.

Because that was what it had been to Amber. That was what that entire period of her life had been, after her father died and her mother had gotten sick. It had been a haze of emotions, of alcohol and every other vice, including sex and kink.

She'd blocked it all out of her mind out of shame. The alcohol had helped with that. But a part of her had remembered it all along. That was why she felt such guilt at seeing Michelle's face.

Amber continued to read, reaching the last page.

I want to go back to that night, that room, and relive it with you, over and over.

Her hands trembling, she placed the letter on the table alongside the photo and sank into the couch behind her. "I don't know what to say…"

She looked up at Carmen, who stood above her, staring back at her with that hard look in her eyes. But behind it was an undercurrent of wariness.

"All of this," she said. "Is it true?"

Amber hesitated. "Yes."

"But you said all along that you didn't know who Michelle was."

"I didn't realize who she was. No, maybe a part of me knew all along."

"I want the truth. Who is this woman?"

Amber bowed her head. "It's exactly as she said. The two of us spent a night together. It was just once, a couple of years ago. I barely remember it. At the time, I was going through a rough patch."

Carmen hesitated. "You mean, after you lost your father?"

Amber nodded. "All I wanted was to drown the pain I felt. And one night, that pain was worse than usual. So I went to a club, Lilith's Den. I got as drunk as I could, and I took a woman back to a hotel room. I forgot all about it until now. I forgot about Michelle."

She glanced at the photo again. "After that night, I never spoke to her again. I'm not proud of it, the way I used her. I feel nothing but shame for that part of my life." Her voice faltered. "I don't remember much from it at all, let alone that one night. That's why I didn't know who she was."

Carmen sat down beside her. "I'm sorry. I didn't know. I shouldn't have jumped to conclusions."

Amber looked at Carmen, realization hitting her. "You thought I lied to you about not knowing who Michelle was."

"Yes, but only for a moment."

Something squeezed inside Amber's chest. Was that why Carmen had been looking at her that way? Because, after everything they'd been through together, she didn't trust her?

"I shouldn't have doubted you," Carmen said. "I know you wouldn't lie to me."

Amber averted her gaze, unable to look her in the eye. "I don't blame you for not trusting me. I'm not someone you should put your trust in. Everything with Michelle just proves it."

"What are you talking about? So you made a mistake. And you weren't in your right mind. If you were too drunk to remember that night, you were too drunk to know what you were doing."

"That doesn't change the fact that I took advantage of her."

"How do you even know you took advantage of her? This woman is delusional, manipulative, and obviously obsessed with you. Maybe she took advantage of you. You were drunk, after all."

Was that a possibility? Thinking back, Amber did remember that it was Michelle who had approached her in the club, not the other way around. Amber rarely let that happen.

But it had been Amber who had gotten the hotel room. It had all been her idea, hadn't it? It was all just a blur.

"That doesn't absolve me of responsibility. Drunk or not, I was the one holding the whip. I was the one in a position of power. Doing the kind of things we did while under the influence was dangerous, stupid, utterly irresponsible of me." She shook her head. "And not just physically. That collar she's always wearing? I gave it to her. It was just for play, just for the night. It wasn't supposed to mean anything. But she obviously didn't see it that way. And I never considered the consequences of such a gesture. I was so careless. And now I'm paying the price."

"You're not blaming yourself for the fact that she's stalking you, are you? For her coming after you? Michelle spent five years in jail for attacking her ex-girlfriend with a knife! She's clearly unstable. None of this is your fault. This letter doesn't change anything."

No, it had changed everything. It had brought all of Amber's shame to light. It had changed the way Carmen saw her. And now, instead of suspicion, Carmen was looking at her with pity.

Amber couldn't stand it any longer.

"I need some time to come to terms with this," she said.

Carmen nodded. "Okay, I'll be in my room if you need me."

"No, I don't mean a few hours. I need time. Space."

"What do you need me to do?"

"The two of us, we've been practically living in each other's pockets for months now. We need some time apart. And it's been weeks since you've had a day off. Why don't you go see your sister?"

Carmen flinched. "What? You can't be serious."

"It will do us both some good. Take a day off, or two. In fact, why don't I call you when I need you? The rest of the team can cover you while you're gone."

"Amber, I know what you're trying to do. You're trying to push me away."

She felt a stabbing in her gut. That was exactly what she was doing. But she needed to be alone. The walls were closing in again, and the other woman's presence was suffocating.

Carmen crossed her arms. "I'm not leaving you."

"I'm not giving you a choice," Amber said.

Carmen's face fell. "What are you saying?"

"I'm telling you to leave."

"Is that an order?"

Amber spoke through gritted teeth. "Yes. It is."

She stood and waited for Carmen to comply. For a

moment, Carmen only stared back at her, a gamut of emotions playing in her eyes. Shock. Disbelief. Hurt.

And finally, resignation.

"Fine," she said. "I'll go. Just remember, if you need me, I'll be there for you. I'm always going to be there for you."

As Carmen left the room, Amber closed her eyes, fighting the urge to call her back as she listened to Carmen's footsteps recede.

CHAPTER 23

Amber arrived at the restaurant where her mother was waiting. Carmen had signed off on the outing because it was all in the name of family, something her bodyguard had always understood the importance of.

But Carmen wasn't here tonight. And Amber wasn't in the mood to reconcile with her mother. She was too consumed with shame and guilt over what she'd learned about the woman stalking her. And she missed Carmen. She felt her absence deeply. She'd become so used to having Carmen by her side.

Instead, she had another member of the security team, Peters, as her personal bodyguard in Carmen's place. The hulking, silent man seemed competent enough. And the rest of the security team was there too, at the entrances, lurking in the restaurant invisibly, as usual. She was safe as could be.

But having Carmen with her wasn't only about security, not anymore.

The maître d' greeted her and led her to her table. Her mother was already seated there.

"Hello, darling," she said.

Amber returned her greeting and took a seat. "How was your doctor's appointment?"

"It went well. Dr. Barnes says everything is looking good. I'm as healthy as a 72-year-old woman with a bad heart could be."

"I'm glad to hear it."

Her mother studied Amber's face, her brows drawing together. "Is everything all right?"

No, she wanted to say. *Nothing is all right.*

But instead, all she said was, "Everything is fine."

"Good," her mother said. "Because I know you wanted to speak to me, but there's something I want to speak to you about too."

"What is it?" Amber couldn't handle any bad news right now.

Her mother clasped her hands together. "The Pryce Foundation Ball. I heard it went well. You did an excellent job with it. I'm impressed."

"Don't sound so surprised, *Mother.* I'm more than capable of hosting a ball." Amber was being harsher than her mother deserved, but she wasn't in the mood for forced civility.

Her mother looked down at her lap. "You're right. I've never given you as much credit as I should. You're a capable woman, and it's time I started treating you as such."

What? No small part of Amber had wanted to hear words like that for years. But why now?

Her stomach dropped. "Is something wrong? Is it your heart? I thought you said you were fine."

Her mother shook her head. "I assure you, I'm perfectly

healthy. But I am getting older. And I want to live out the rest of my days at a slower pace. So I've made a decision. I'm retiring from public life. I'm retiring from my position on the company's board, and from running the Pryce Foundation. I'm leaving it all in your hands."

Amber blinked. "What? Are you sure?"

"I'm sure. You're ready. But if you don't think you are—"

"No, I am. I can handle this. I just didn't think you thought I could."

"Why wouldn't I?"

Amber stared at her, incredulous. "Why wouldn't you? Because every time we talk, you make it clear that I don't live up to your expectations!"

Her mother frowned. "Do you really think that?"

"How could I not? You don't approve of me. Of how I live my life, of who I love, who I am. It's obvious you're disappointed in me. Ashamed of me, even."

"Oh, Amber. I'm so sorry. I never meant to make you feel that way." Her mother's voice quavered. "But I can see how I have. I know I've always put so much pressure on you, but you've always impressed me with how well you've managed it. And I'm so proud of everything you've become. I couldn't have asked for a better daughter."

"Then why are you constantly trying to make me into someone I'm not? To make me fit this idea you have about what my life should be? You keep telling me how I need to settle down, get married, have children, all so I can live up to this legacy of yours."

"That's not what that's about. When I say those things, it's not about my legacy, it's about yours. I just want you to be happy."

Amber scoffed. "I find that hard to believe."

"It's the truth. Amber, two years ago, I lost your father, and then I found out I have a life-threatening heart condition. And now, I've finally been given a clean bill of health, a second chance, and it's made me realize how precious life is. It made me think about what really matters, what I want to have achieved, what I want to leave behind when I'm gone. It made me realize what's important to me. And that's family."

She reached across the table and clasped Amber's hands in hers. "I know I spent most of your life teaching you to stand on your own two feet, to not need anyone else. And because of that, you grew up strong and independent, and I couldn't be prouder. But I made a mistake in teaching you that and that alone. Yes, it's important to be strong. But what's more important is love."

Love? Family? Of all the things this cold, distant woman cared about, it was love that she treasured?

"Of all my achievements in this life, you are the one I'll always be proudest of," her mother said. "I love you more than anyone else on this earth, and I feel so blessed to have raised you and watched you grow. And I want that for you. I want you to experience what that kind of love feels like. Maybe not in a child, but in someone you can call family. A partner you can build a life with, and enjoy that life together."

"And I want that, Mom. I understand, I do. But I'm not going to find that the way you want me to. Not with a man. It will be with someone I love. A woman."

Her mother was silent for a moment. "I know. And I accept that. I should have accepted it a long time ago. I was just too set in my ways. And I find it hard to believe that you won't have children."

"Is that what this is about? Children?" Amber let out an exasperated sigh. "It's the 21st century. If I want children, I can have them with whoever I want. I can even have them by myself. But if I do, it will be my way, and my choice."

"You're right. I don't care how you go about it. I just don't want you to be alone. Everybody needs someone. Even us Pryce women. We can't do it on our own. Especially not you."

Amber crossed her arms. "What's that supposed to mean?"

"This is exactly what I mean. You're a Pryce through and through, as stubborn as you are determined. You need someone who is patient enough to put up with that, but forceful enough to call you out when you're being unreasonable, to give you the tough love you need. Someone kind, who you'll be able to let your guard down with, but who's strong enough to support you when you need it. Someone loyal, who will be by your side always, so that on those rare occasions when you can't be strong, they will be there for you."

Amber's stomach stirred. Wasn't there someone who fit that description? Someone loyal, dependable, strong?

And she had pushed her away, all so that she could wallow in her shame, alone.

"You need someone," her mother said. "And I don't want to leave this earth knowing I failed you by not teaching you that. So promise me. Promise me you'll find someone."

"That's the thing," Amber said. "I've already found her."

"You have?"

"I think so, but I..." Amber shook her head. "I'm sorry. I can't explain it now, but you're right. There's something I need to do, something I need to make right." She squeezed her mother's hands. "But thank you. Thank you for telling me how you feel. And thank you for trusting me with your legacy. I won't let you down."

"I know you won't."

"Will you excuse me? I need to go do something. It will only take a moment."

Her mother nodded. "Go right ahead. I'll be here."

Amber left the table and headed toward the restrooms. She needed to collect herself before making the phone call.

As she reached the bathroom, she noticed her bodyguard trailing behind her closely. Peters stopped, seemingly unsure of whether to go inside with her or not.

"It's called the *ladies'* room," she snapped. "Wait outside."

Peters gave her a nod, his relief palpable. He seemed the opposite of Carmen. She'd always bristled at being told what to do, and had only ever obeyed Amber grudgingly. She wasn't a pushover. And she wasn't afraid to call Amber out. She'd always been stubbornly loyal, even when Amber didn't deserve it.

Amber needed to get her back.

She slipped into the bathroom and walked over to the vanity. Placing her purse down on the counter, she took a moment to gather herself, then took out her phone.

As she pulled up Carmen's number, a stall door opened behind her. She glanced up at it through the mirror. Her blood ran cold.

Standing in the stall was a familiar woman. Black hair. Dark eyes. A collar around her neck.

Michelle.

Heart thumping, Amber swung around to face her. Her elbow bumped her purse, knocking it to the ground, its contents spilling onto the floor with a clatter. But picking her things up was the last thing on Amber's mind.

She glanced toward the door.

"No." Michelle's voice was sharp and firm. "Don't move."

It was then that Amber noticed the woman was holding something in her hand. She froze.

It was a gun.

Michelle pointed it at Amber's chest. "Drop the phone and turn around."

Amber cursed internally. She'd forgotten about the phone in her hand. And it was too late to use it now.

Slowly, she put the phone down and turned her back to Michelle, raising her arms as she did. "What do you want?"

"What do you think?" Michelle said. "You've been getting my letters, haven't you?"

Amber nodded. "Yes."

"Then you know exactly what I want. You." She stepped toward Amber, pressing the gun into her back. "You're going to come with me now."

Amber glanced at the door again.

"Not that way." Michelle tipped her head toward the window at the far end of the room. "Through there."

She prodded Amber's back with the gun, steering her toward the window. It was just large enough for a person to fit through.

She unlatched the window and opened it, then prodded Amber again. "Go on."

Amber stuck her head through the window. Outside was an alley, completely deserted. Could she make a run for it?

Michelle raised the gun to Amber's head. "Don't even think about it. I've waited years for this chance. I'm *not* letting you get away."

Amber's stomach iced over. The detached coldness in the woman's voice told her that she meant what she said.

"This is your final warning. *Move.*"

Amber looked back at the bathroom one last time.

Then, she took a deep breath and stepped through the window.

CHAPTER 24

"Hey." Jo sat down next to Carmen on the couch. "Do you want to watch a movie?"

"Sure," Carmen replied. "You pick something."

Jo frowned. "Is everything okay with you? Ever since you came home, you've been all mopey."

"I'm fine. It's just this job, it's been a stressful one."

It had been a few days since she'd left the Pryce residence and returned home. Amber had wanted space, and time. Carmen was respecting her wishes and giving her both.

But how much time did she need, exactly? Carmen hadn't heard a word from her. Did she even have a job anymore? Amber hadn't explicitly fired her, but she'd made it clear she wanted her gone. Was it only temporary, or was it for good?

But Carmen didn't care about the job, or the money. All she cared about was Amber. And the longer they were apart, the wider the gulf between them felt.

Was everything between them damaged irreparably?

She should never have reacted to that letter the way she had. She couldn't stop thinking about the way Amber's eyes had filled with pain when she realized Carmen thought she'd lied to her.

Why had Carmen believed the words of a delusional stalker instead of trusting Amber?

Beside her, Jo spoke up. "Wanna talk about it?"

"No, it's just boring work stuff," Carmen said. "Now, are you going to choose a movie?"

Jo crossed her arms. "I'm not an idiot, you know. Do you really think I can't tell when something is wrong with you? Do you think I can't see that something's eating you up inside? I'm your sister. And I'm not a kid. You can talk to me. Let me be there for you, just like you're always here for me."

Carmen sighed. Her sister was right.

But before she could say anything, her phone began to ring. It was Wheeler. Was it about Amber?

She gave Jo an apologetic look. "Hold that thought."

She picked up the call and headed into the other room. "Wheeler, what's going on?"

"I have some bad news," he said. "It's Pryce. She's gone."

Carmen's heart plummeted from her chest. "What do you mean, gone?"

"She disappeared. She went out to dinner. The team went with her, and we did everything to the letter, but we took our eyes off her for just a few seconds, and she was gone."

"What? Did someone take her? Was it Glover?"

"We don't know, but it's likely. We found Pryce's purse in the ladies' room, with everything inside it strewn over the floor. Her phone was left behind, too. If she went somewhere, it wasn't willingly."

Carmen cursed. It had to be Michelle. She'd finally gotten to Amber.

"We've contacted the police," he said. "They're looking into it, and so are we. But we don't have a lot to go on. We need to figure out where Glover could have taken her. Do you have any ideas?"

Carmen thought for a moment. Then, it hit her. The last letter Michelle had sent. It had ended in a sentence that had seemed disturbingly aggressive. It had been a threat.

I want to go back to that night, that room, and relive it with you, over and over.

"The hotel," she said. "Glover, she must have taken Amber to the hotel."

"What hotel?" Wheeler asked.

"The one she wrote about in her last letter. I don't have time to explain it, but there was some truth in that letter. Glover wanted to recreate that night."

"Do you know which hotel it was?"

"No idea," Carmen said. "But it was somewhere in the city. And probably a five-star place, since it was Amber who paid for the hotel room."

"There have to be dozens of five-star hotels in the city. We can't check them all."

"You're right. We need to narrow it down more. I'll think about it, try to figure something out. In the meantime, send the rest of the team out to start looking at the closest potential locations. Have them talk to the staff, find out if they noticed anything suspicious. It's getting late, so most hotels will be operating on a skeleton crew, but someone has to have seen Amber Pryce strolling through the doors."

Not that Amber would have done so willingly. Was she being physically forced, restrained? Held at knifepoint by Michelle, just like she'd done to her ex-girlfriend? The thought chilled her.

She had to find Amber before it was too late.

After some back and forth with Wheeler, Carmen told him she'd meet him at the Pryce residence before hanging up the phone.

As she left the room, she ran into Jo in the hallway.

"Is everything okay?" Jo asked.

"Work emergency," Carmen replied. "I need to go."

"Did something happen to Amber?"

"How did you... you were eavesdropping, weren't you?"

Jo shrugged. "Just a little. What's going on? If you tell me, maybe I can help."

"How, Jo? There's nothing you could possibly do!" Carmen rubbed her temples. "I'm sorry, I shouldn't have snapped at you. I'm just stressed out."

"It's okay. I don't know what I can do, but maybe if you tell me what's going on, I can help somehow. In case you've forgotten, I know how to do certain things. Like, I could trace her phone."

Carmen narrowed her eyes. "How do you know how to..." She shook her head. "I don't want to know. And it doesn't matter. Amber doesn't have her phone with her. And you're not doing anything illegal. No hacking into anything."

But Carmen was desperate. And maybe there was something her sister could do to help.

"Here's the deal." She explained the situation with Amber, leaving out some of the more risqué details. "So what I need is to narrow the options down. It'll take us too long to search every five-star hotel in the city."

"Hm." Jo's brows drew together in thought. "Do you know anything else about the hotel? Like a general location?"

"Nope. Amber was vague about what happened that night. We have a photo taken inside the room, but it doesn't show much."

"A photo? Can I see it?"

"Sure. I'll have someone send it to me."

Carmen shot off a quick text to Wheeler. Within minutes, he replied, a scanned copy of the photo attached.

She showed it to Jo. "Here. Er, it's a bit racy."

Jo examined the picture, her eyebrows raising as she saw the toys on the bed. "I'm not going to ask what's going on here, but one day you're going to tell me." She pinched the photo on the screen, zooming in. "We can use this."

"How?"

"Look at the room in the background. The wallpaper, the furniture, it's really distinctive. We can see if it matches any photos of hotels in the area online."

"That's assuming there are photos of that exact room on the internet. And it will take too long to look through all of them."

"Not if we use a script," Jo said.

"A what?"

"It's a computer program. We can make it look through the photos for us and let us know if there are any matches."

"You mean, like a facial recognition program, but for backgrounds?"

Jo nodded. "Basically. But this won't just search a specific database. It'll search all the photos on the internet, including social media. We can limit the script to photos taken in the city limits based on social media tags and EXIF data. That's the metadata all digital photos have telling you the time, date, and location a photo was taken, among other things."

Carmen frowned. "That seems invasive."

Jo shrugged. "If you're silly enough to upload your vacation snaps to social media without stripping the EXIF data, you obviously don't care about privacy."

"I don't know. Is this all legal? You're 18 now, you can't get in any trouble with the law or you'll get a record."

"It's totally legal, I promise. Do you want to find Amber, or not?"

Jo was right. With Amber's life at stake, Carmen couldn't afford to hesitate. "How long will it take?"

"Not long. I don't have to write a whole script, I'll just grab one from a repository online and adjust the parameters. Then we let the program do its thing. Should take a couple of hours, give or take."

That was quicker than searching every five-star hotel in the city. "Okay," Carmen said. "Do it. I'll call the team and let them know what's going on."

Carmen paced the living room, raising a hand to stifle a yawn. It was getting late. And every minute that passed was a minute that Amber was in danger.

She checked her phone. Still no word from Wheeler, or any of the others. She'd decided to wait at home instead of going to the Pryce residence. Her house was more centrally located, and it would be easier to chase up Amber from here. The rest of the security team weren't at the house, anyway. They were scattered around the city, searching for Amber.

She glanced at Jo, who sat curled up at one end of the couch with her laptop. That program of hers hadn't gotten any hits yet.

Carmen's stomach churned. She should never have left Amber alone like she did. She should have never let Amber push her away. Amber hadn't given her a choice at the time, but Carmen shouldn't have listened to her. Amber was stubborn, the only person she knew who was more stubborn than herself. Carmen should have refused to leave her side.

"Can you stop pacing around like that?" Jo said. "You're making me nervous."

"Sorry." Carmen sat down on the couch. "Any hits yet?"

"Still nothing, but it's still early."

Carmen sighed.

Jo put her laptop down and unfolded her legs. "You're really worried about her, aren't you?"

"Of course I am. She's my..." *Client*, Carmen wanted to say. But Amber wasn't just her client anymore.

"Your what?"

Carmen shook her head. "I don't know. I don't know what Amber is to me. She isn't just my client. She hasn't been in a long time."

"So you're friends? Or..." Jo's eyes widened. "Wait, is there something going on between the two of you?"

"We've been… seeing each other." Carmen wasn't about to share all the explicit details with her sister.

"Oh my god. You and Amber Pryce? I knew it!"

"Don't get too excited. The last time we spoke, things between us were tense. And now she's in the hands of a deranged stalker." Something clenched inside Carmen's chest. "I should have never let my feelings get in the way of doing my job. If I hadn't, she wouldn't be in danger right now. But at the same time, I can't stop thinking about how I never told her how I feel."

"It's not too late for that. You can still tell her how you feel, right after you rescue her."

"This isn't one of your rom-coms," Carmen said. "This is real life. And if we don't find her soon…" It had been hours since Michelle had taken her. What if they were too late?

"You're going to find her. You can't give up now. And you can't give up on her. I don't know what happened between you two, but I've never seen you care this much about anyone other than me. You have to find her, and you have to fix things with her. This is your chance to go after something that makes *you* happy, for once in your life."

"You're… you're right."

"I know I am. How many times do I have to tell you that I'm not a kid? I see the way you live your life. I always have. All you do is make sacrifices for others. It's time you started living for yourself."

Carmen stared at her. "Wow, you really aren't a kid anymore. I'm sorry for treating you that way, seeing you that way. It was never about you, not really. It was about me. A part of me just doesn't want to see you grow up. Because if you're an adult, that means I can't protect you anymore."

"But I don't need protecting."

"I know. I see that. I guess I just want to keep you safe to make up for the past."

"What do you mean?"

Carmen hesitated. She'd never spoken to Jo about her role in their parents' deaths, but perhaps now was the time. "It's about the night that Mom and Dad died. I know you don't remember it."

Jo shrugged. "Not really. But Abuelita told me what happened. You hid me. You kept me safe."

"Not exactly. I tried, but in the end, it was me who gave us away. One of the men hurt Mom, and I got scared. I screamed, and then Dad tried to protect us. That's why they killed him and Mom."

"I didn't know all that." Jo paused. "Wait, do you think I blame you for what happened to Mom and Dad? Or is it yourself that you blame? That's it, isn't it?"

"If I'd just stayed quiet, our parents would still be around. You'd have had a normal childhood."

Jo shook her head. "You don't know that. You don't know what might or might not have happened. But none of that matters, because it's not your fault Mom and Dad died. And I could never blame you for what happened to them. I'm grateful to you for taking care of me, that night and ever since. And if this is the reason you've been living the way you have all this time, focusing on me and not yourself, you need to stop thinking like that. You need to let go of the past, of this idea that you have to protect me. You need to move on and start living your life."

"You're right," Carmen said. "I should have talked to you about all this sooner, but I've been underestimating you.

And under-appreciating you. I'm so grateful to have you too. I couldn't have asked for a better sister. Thank you for being there for me."

Jo smiled. "Anytime. And now that you're finally convinced that I'm an adult, does this mean you'll let me go to Stanford?"

Carmen nodded. "You can go to Stanford. You can go anywhere you want. Just as long as you stay out of trouble."

"I'll try. Thanks, Carmen."

She threw her arms around Carmen's neck. Carmen held her tight. Who knew when her little sister would let her hug her like this again?

Beside them, Jo's laptop pinged.

"Is that what I think it is?" Carmen asked.

Jo nodded and grabbed the laptop. Carmen held her breath. Did they have a match?

"Looks like it's found something. Here." Jo turned the screen toward Carmen. "The background matches this photo taken at The Grand Star. It's helpfully tagged the penthouse suite."

"That has to be where Amber is." Carmen stood up. "Can you send the address to my phone?"

Jo nodded. "Go get her."

Carmen grabbed her gun from the safe in her bedroom, holstering it around her waist before leaving the house. As she headed to her car, she called Wheeler.

"I think I know where Amber is," she told him. "The Grand Star, in the penthouse suite. I'm on my way now, it isn't far from me. It's a long shot, but it's all we've got."

"I'll call the rest of the team, have them back you up," Wheeler said.

"Don't. I might be wrong, so I need everyone else to keep looking for her, just in case."

"Understood. But you still need backup. I've got some of the others with me. We'll meet you there. *Do not* go in without us."

"Sorry, but I'm not waiting. Not when Amber is in danger."

She hung up, ignoring Wheeler's protests, and got into her car. She couldn't afford to wait any longer. She needed to get to Amber before it was too late.

CHAPTER 25

Amber balled her fists behind her back and pulled her wrists apart, attempting to loosen the ropes binding them. They weren't budging.

She let out a frustrated sigh. How long had it been since Michelle had brought her here? After she'd climbed out the window at the restaurant, Michelle had ushered her into a car before driving them to the hotel's parking garage and sneaking Amber up to the penthouse suite at gunpoint. Amber had hoped they'd cross paths with someone so she could sound the alarm, but other than a frustratingly distracted bellboy, no one had noticed them. There were disadvantages to the high-class hotel's unwritten policy of discretion when it came to late-night guests.

She craned her neck, peering down the back of the chair over her shoulder. The ropes weren't budging. She cursed. Michelle wouldn't be in the bathroom for much longer. Even if Amber managed to free her wrists, she'd have to free her ankles too, which were tied to the legs of the chair.

Perhaps if she had something sharp, she could cut the

ropes instead. She glanced around the room, but she couldn't see anything that could help her, let alone anything within reach. The chair she was bound to, made of wood too sturdy to break, sat several feet away from any other furniture. On the bed nearby was a collection of restraints, whips, and toys, just like in that photo.

Michelle had painstakingly recreated every detail from that night, right down to the bottle of expensive liquor they'd been drinking. She'd remembered everything, obsessed over everything, all this time. The depth of her preoccupation with Amber was terrifying.

In the adjoining bathroom, a toilet flushed. Amber whispered a curse. Michelle would return to the room any minute now. Amber looked over her shoulder, pulling at the ropes again. She needed to escape before it was too late.

"Stop that."

Amber froze. Slowly, she looked up to find Michelle standing in the bathroom doorway, the collar around her neck and her gun held casually in one hand, the dark shadow hanging over her eyes sending panic surging through Amber's body.

She pushed it down. She needed to keep it together if she was going to get through this.

"There's no point struggling. I tied those knots perfectly." Michelle sauntered over to Amber's chair, looming over her menacingly. "After that night we spent together, I learned to do what you do. I learned how to tie someone up so they couldn't escape. I learned how to make pain pleasurable. I learned how to make pain *hurt*."

Amber's heart hammered against the inside of her chest. Michelle turned to the bed beside them, reaching for a flogger that lay on top of it. It wasn't the kind that Amber used in the bedroom. It was more akin to a cat-o'-nine-tails, with heavy beads knotted into the ends of each tail. It was designed to do damage, to cause pain beyond the limits of even the most extreme of masochists.

The tools laid out on the bed weren't tools of pleasure. They were tools of torture.

And that scared her more than the gun in Michelle's hand.

Amber steeled herself. She needed to find a way out of this. And if she couldn't free herself on her own, she'd need to go through Michelle.

"Look," Amber said. "If you tell me what you want, maybe we can work something out."

"I already told you what I want," Michelle said. "I want us to be together again, just like that night."

Amber stifled a curse. They'd gone back and forth like this several times already, but she needed to keep trying. "And I'm right here with you. So if you just untie me—"

Michelle shook her head, abandoning the flogger. "No. *No.* You don't understand. I don't want it to be like last time. This time, I want you to feel what I felt. Not just that night, but every night, every waking moment since."

"And what is it that you felt? What is it you feel?" It was a dangerous line of questioning to go down, but it was all Amber had. "Tell me what you feel."

"Isn't it obvious? After all those letters I wrote to you. After I poured my heart out to you!"

"You're... in love with me."

"But it's so much more than that. It's so much more than just love. I've idolized you for years. I've watched you for so long. When I learned about that club you liked to go to, Lilith's Den, I spent months just trying to get in. And then I waited for you there, every night for weeks."

Amber's stomach lurched. That had been two years ago. Michelle had been obsessed with her for that long? The two of them meeting in the club, the two of them coming to this hotel room that night, hadn't been chance. Michelle had orchestrated it all, and Amber had been too preoccupied with her grief to notice she was being manipulated.

"So when you finally walked through those doors, it was like fate," Michelle said. "We were meant to be. That night we shared just proved it. You're my soulmate."

Staring deep into Amber's eyes, Michelle reached out and stroked her cheek. Amber flinched. Too late, she realized her mistake.

Michelle's face clouded over. She slipped her finger under the collar around her neck, pulling at it violently. "You gave me this. You made me *yours*. I thought for sure that we were going to be together. But after that night, I never heard a word from you."

"I know," Amber said. "And I'm sorry for the way I treated you that night. I was going through a rough time, and I used you to numb the pain I felt. It was a mistake. I'm only human. But that's no excuse. I'm sorry I hurt you."

Michelle's eyes glistened with tears. "I've waited so long to hear you say that. And I could never hold it against you. I just want to be with you. And now that that's out of the way, we can finally be together."

Amber swallowed. *If I lie, string her along, I might get out of this.* But where would lying lead her? What would Michelle expect from her?

Could she even bring herself to pretend when her heart belonged to someone else?

She almost laughed at the absurdity of it. All it took was facing down a deranged stalker at gunpoint for her to admit to herself what she felt for Carmen. Her bodyguard, the very person she'd hired to prevent something like this from happening.

And she would be safe by Carmen's side right now, if she hadn't pushed her away.

Amber's regret must have shown on her face.

"You still don't believe it," Michelle said. "You don't believe we're soulmates. That's why I had to bring you here. I have to show you that we're meant to be. But it doesn't matter if you believe me or not. Because even if you don't, I'm going to make sure that the two of us will be together, *forever.*"

The implications of Michelle's words were clear. And all Amber could think about was that she was going to die without ever telling Carmen how she felt.

Gun in hand, Michelle turned back to the bed, surveying her tools of torture. A chill rolled down Amber's body. Michelle wasn't going to end this quickly. She was going to draw it out, torment her.

At least that would give Amber time. But what was the point of time when all hope was lost?

She closed her eyes and took a deep breath, then another. *Stay calm. Focus...*

Her ears pricked. *What was that?* A faint click, coming from the direction of the door.

She turned her head slightly, glancing toward it. The door had opened, just a crack. And that crack was growing wider.

Someone was here to rescue her!

She looked at Michelle. The woman hadn't noticed anything. Breath frozen in her chest, Amber watched out of the corner of her eye as the door opened wider…

Suddenly, it made a loud creak. Michelle spun around to look at it. Amber's heart dropped.

Her savior had been caught.

Apparently realizing this, they burst into the room. It was Carmen. She was dressed in her leather jacket, a cold, focused look in her eyes and a gun in her hands, pointed directly at Michelle.

But Michelle was faster. Before Amber knew it, the barrel of her gun was pressed against her temple.

Michelle addressed Carmen. "Don't move."

Carmen froze in place, her eyes flitting between Amber and Michelle. "I just want to talk," she said. "Why don't you put the gun down and—"

"Nice try, but I'm the one who has Amber's life in my hands. You're going to put your gun down, not me."

"Why don't we—"

"Gun. Down. Now. Or I'll blow Amber's brains out. Don't think I won't do it."

Carmen hesitated. Amber could see the calculations racing through the Marine's head. Could she take out Michelle before the woman pulled the trigger?

"Okay. I'm putting it down." Carmen held up her hands, then crouched down slowly, placing the gun on the floor.

Amber cursed to herself, her relief turning to dread. Carmen was in danger now too, and all because of her.

"Slide it over here," Michelle said. "And put your hands up where I can see them."

Carmen obeyed, sliding the gun over to her. Her own gun still pointed at Amber's head, Michelle leaned down and picked it up, placing it on the side table behind her.

Silently, Carmen took a few steps toward them, stopping as Michelle turned back around.

She didn't seem to notice that Carmen had gotten closer. "You. Why do you look so familiar?" She tilted her head, studying Carmen's face. "You're the bodyguard. You're the reason I couldn't get close to Amber. You've been following her around ever since that stupid auction."

The charity auction. Had it been Michelle in the car that had almost run Amber over? So her intuition had been right. And so had Carmen's.

"Do you have any idea how long I've been waiting for you to leave her alone? And now you're here, messing up my plans again." Michelle looked at the bed, at the tools laid out there, before cocking the gun at Amber again. "Looks like I'll have to skip straight to ending this."

Terror seized Amber's body. She was so close to freedom. It couldn't end here, not like this.

"You don't want to do that," Carmen said. With an unnerving smoothness, she took a few more steps toward them. "Let's talk about this."

Michelle finally seemed to realize Carmen was creeping forward. "Stop. Don't come any closer."

"Okay." Carmen put her hands up higher. "I'll stay right here. But let's talk this through. I'm unarmed. I can't hurt you."

"What is there to talk about?" Michelle said.

"Let's talk about why you're doing this. I know you don't want to hurt her, not really."

"How would you know?" Michelle snapped. "You don't know what I want, what I *feel*."

"I think I do. You say you love her."

"I love her so much it hurts. That's why I need to make the pain stop." The gun began to shake in Michelle's hand. "And I need to make sure we're together forever."

Carmen took another step forward. "But can't you see the pain you're causing her? If you love her, why would you want to hurt her?"

"I…" Michelle looked at her gun, then at Amber, her face contorting with confusion.

Then, it was replaced with anger.

Her head swiveled to face Carmen. "How do you know that I love her?" She turned back to Amber. "She knows about us?"

But before she could respond, Carmen spoke.

"I do," she said, inching forward again. She was only a few steps from Michelle now. "I know everything."

Michelle wheeled around to face Carmen, pointing the gun at her once again. But Carmen didn't flinch. She only looked more determined.

Then it hit Amber. This was exactly what Carmen wanted. She was trying to draw Michelle's attention away from Amber. She was putting herself in Michelle's crosshairs on purpose.

"Carmen, stop," Amber cried.

"Shut up," Michelle snapped.

"Let's just calm down," Carmen said.

Michelle shook her head. "No. I need to know. How did you know about us?"

"I read your letters," Carmen said. "I know everything."

"Those letters were private!" Michelle turned to Amber, pointing the gun at her again. "How could you show them to her?"

"I read your letters," Carmen repeated. "So I could keep you from getting to her. Because I wanted her for myself."

"What?" Michelle looked at Carmen but kept the gun pointed at Amber. "Are you saying… are you…"

Carmen nodded. "That's right. I'm in love with Amber. So if you want her, you'll have to go through me."

Amber's stomach flipped. Of all the stupid things Carmen could say, she was saying this?

She took a step toward Michelle. Michelle swung the gun, pointing it at Carmen's head, her hands trembling. "Don't come any closer!"

But Carmen was already within arm's reach. And Amber could see in her eyes what she intended to do.

"No," Amber whispered.

Carmen kept her eyes fixed on Michelle, but her next words were directed to Amber. "I need you to trust me."

It all happened at once. Moving faster than seemed humanly possible, Carmen seized Michelle by the wrist, jerking the gun upward and tackling her to the ground.

But Michelle didn't let go of the gun. The two women wrestled on the floor, the gun held between them as they grappled for it. Michelle threw her elbow inward, smashing it into the side of Carmen's face. But Carmen didn't flinch. And she didn't let go of her grip on Michelle's wrist, even as Michelle clawed and kicked at her.

Amber watched them struggle, her heart in her throat. She needed to do something, anything, to help, but she was still tied to the damn chair.

Suddenly, the gun went off. Amber's chest seized, her ears ringing as the sound echoed through the room.

But Carmen and Michelle didn't stop moving, didn't stop struggling. The bullet had missed its mark.

And the kickback gave Carmen the opening she needed. She wrenched the gun from Michelle's hand, then raised it up high and slammed the grip against her temple.

Michelle fell still.

Amber let out a breath. It was over.

Carmen rose to her feet slowly, the gun pointed at Michelle. When it became clear she wasn't moving, Carmen disarmed the gun and set it aside before grabbing her own gun from the table. Holstering it at her hip, she rushed over to where Amber sat tied to the chair.

She took Amber's face in her hands, looking furiously into her eyes. "Are you all right? Are you hurt?"

"I'm fine." Amber's voice shook. "She didn't hurt me. Please, get me out of these ropes."

Reaching into her pocket, Carmen pulled out a knife and cut through the ropes binding Amber's wrists and ankles. As soon as she was free, Amber stood up and embraced her savior with all her strength.

"Thank god you came when you did," she said. "How did you know I was here?"

"It's a long story," Carmen replied. "I'm just glad I found you. I'm never leaving your side again."

"And I'm never leaving yours. I'm so sorry for pushing

you away." She pulled Carmen's face to hers and planted a desperate kiss on her lips. "Let's get out of here."

Carmen nodded. "Just give me a moment to catch my breath." She drew away, leaning down on the back of the chair beside her. "I feel a little light-headed."

Amber frowned. Carmen did look pale. As she reached for Carmen's arm to support her, Amber noticed a growing dark patch on Carmen's leather jacket at the shoulder. There was a small hole in the center of it...

Amber's heart sank. The bullet hadn't missed its mark. "You've been shot."

Carmen looked down at her shoulder, blinking. "Oh."

What little color that remained on her face drained from it. Then, her knees gave way, and she collapsed to the floor.

"No, no, no..." Amber pulled back Carmen's jacket and pressed her hands against the wound. "Carmen. *Carmen!*"

But her eyes were closed. And there was so much blood.

She looked around frantically. She needed to call for help, but she couldn't leave Carmen's side. And with every passing moment, Carmen was losing more blood, her life slipping through Amber's fingertips.

A scream tore through her chest. She couldn't lose Carmen, not after everything.

Not before she had a chance to tell her how she felt.

Suddenly, heavy footsteps began pounding in the hallway outside. A second later, the room filled with people. Wheeler. Hudson, all the others.

One of them called for an ambulance. And as another stepped in to staunch Carmen's wound, the faint sound of sirens reached Amber's ears.

CHAPTER 26

Carmen opened her eyes, then slammed them shut again. The light was too harsh, too painful. Her head felt like it was stuffed with cotton wool. And with every breath, something pulled in the side of her chest.

She inhaled slowly, pushing through it as she attempted to make sense of her surroundings. She was lying down, on something soft. A bed. But where was she? And what was that beeping sound? There was something stuck into her arm, too.

Was she in a hospital? She opened her eyes again, slowly this time. As her vision adjusted, the fog in her head cleared, her memory returning. She'd gone to the hotel, she'd found Amber, she'd disarmed Michelle, and had set Amber free. At some point, she'd been shot, which explained why she was in a hospital bed. But that wasn't all that had happened…

Had she told Amber she loved her?

She sat upright. At least, she tried to. But her head felt heavy, and her shoulder ached. And before she knew it, she was sinking back down to the bed.

She groaned.

Suddenly, someone was beside her, holding her hand. "Don't try to move."

Carmen turned her head. Amber was sitting at her bedside, her face lined with fatigue, her hair pulled back in a simple ponytail. She looked like she hadn't slept in days. And she was wearing a sweatshirt. Amber Pryce owned sweatshirts? They'd lived together for months, and Carmen had never seen her in one.

Yet, she looked more beautiful than ever.

Carmen smiled. She couldn't think of anyone she'd rather have by her side.

Amber scowled. "What are you smiling about? Do you have any idea how lucky you are to be alive? If that bullet had hit you just an inch to the right, you'd be dead!"

"Good thing it didn't," Carmen croaked.

Amber stood up and glowered down at her. "How can you be so casual about this? I can't believe you. Putting yourself in harm's way like that, provoking an armed madwoman to draw attention away from me? She could have killed you!"

"You didn't seem to mind at the time."

"That was before I noticed you'd been shot. You are unbelievable. You're so stubborn, so reckless, so..." Amber's voice cracked. "I thought I'd lost you."

Carmen stared up at her. Were those tears in her eyes? As they spilled onto Amber's cheeks, Carmen's heart squeezed.

"I..." She tried to sit up again, earning a sharp look from Amber.

"I told you not to move," she snapped.

Carmen lay back down.

"I almost lost you," Amber repeated, glaring at her through tears. "You almost *died* because of me. So you're going to lie in that bed, even if I have to tie you to it, and you're going to get better. And when we leave this hospital, together, I'm going to nurse you back to health." Her hands clenched into fists. "And even when you've recovered, I'm never, ever going to leave your side, because I love you."

Carmen's pulse sped up. "You... love me?"

"Yes, and like the fool I am, I didn't realize it until I had a gun pointed at my head. At that moment, all I could think about was how I'd give anything to see your face again, to hear your voice, to hold you in my arms one more time. How if I died there and then, I'd never get the chance to tell you how I feel. So I've been sitting here for god knows how many days and nights, waiting for you to wake up, just so I could tell you that!"

"I—"

"And I heard what you said in that hotel room. Don't tell me you were just trying to distract Michelle. Don't blame it on adrenaline. I know what I heard. I felt it in your voice. Please, just this once, be honest with your feelings and stop holding everything back—"

Carmen raised a hand weakly. "You don't have to convince me. Sure, what I said back then was in the heat of the moment, but my words were true. I won't deny it. I won't deny my feelings any longer. I'm not turning away from what makes me happy. I love you too."

Amber smiled. She leaned down, cupped Carmen's face in her palm, and kissed her gently, her tears wet on Carmen's cheeks.

But a second later, she pulled away. "We need to stop. You're not supposed to be exerting yourself."

"This hardly counts as exertion," Carmen said. "I feel fine."

"I'm sure you do, given all the painkillers you're on." Amber crossed her arms. "You were shot, for god's sake. You lost a ton of blood, and you had to have surgery to remove the bullet and close the wound. You've been out for days. You're not fine."

Carmen grimaced. "Was it that bad?"

"Yes, it was that bad. But the good news is, the doctors expect you to make a full recovery. The bad news is, you'll have to rest up for a very long time. And I wasn't joking about tying you to the bed. If you don't rest, I will not hesitate to do so."

"I'm sure that won't be necessary."

"Then you don't know yourself very well."

Suddenly, a thought occurred to Carmen. "Jo. Where is she? You said I've been out for days? Did someone tell her I'm here? Does she know I'm okay?"

Amber placed her hand on Carmen's arm. "Don't panic. Jo is being taken care of. She refused to leave your room this entire time, but after she nearly collapsed from exhaustion, I booked her a room in a hotel nearby so she could get some sleep. It took some convincing to get her to leave though. Apparently, stubbornness runs in the family."

"Thank you. I appreciate you looking out for her."

Amber nodded. "I'll give her a call to let her know you've woken up. The two of us have become quite close over the past few days. She told me all about how she helped you find me. She's a smart girl. Sweet, too."

"A woman. And yes, she is."

"You did a wonderful job raising her." Amber stood up. "I'll go call her."

"Wait," Carmen said. "What happened after I passed out? What happened to Michelle?"

"Well, the rest of your team showed up, followed by an ambulance and the police. They arrested Michelle, and she's in jail awaiting charges. Stalking, harassment, abduction, possession of an illegal firearm, among other things. She's going away for a long time. And it's for the best, given her history. I hope she can get the help she needs too."

"And how are you feeling about all this?"

"Mostly relieved that the ordeal is over. For months now, she's been lurking in the background. For months, I felt like I couldn't breathe. But now I can, all thanks to you."

Carmen smiled. "I'm glad."

Amber leaned down and kissed her on the cheek. "Now, you're looking a little too peaky for my liking, so I'm going to go find a doctor and then call your sister." She gave Carmen a stern look. "Promise me that you'll rest while I'm gone, okay?"

Carmen nodded. Rest sounded pretty good right now. "I will."

CHAPTER 27

A mber watched from the second-floor window as Carmen said goodbye to her sister outside. Jo had come by to visit her at the Pryce residence.

It had been more than a month since Carmen had been discharged from the hospital, and Amber had insisted she move in while she recuperated. Ostensibly, it was so Amber could take care of her. But in reality, after everything they'd been through together, Amber simply couldn't bear the thought of being apart from her for one second.

Luckily, Carmen felt the same way. At first, she'd been nervous about telling everyone about the two of them. But apparently, her colleagues had all figured it out already, and her sister was on board with the relationship too.

Surprisingly, so was Amber's mother. She was mostly just pleased that Amber had finally found someone, so pleased that she'd resumed nagging Amber about getting married. While it was much too soon for that, Amber didn't doubt that Carmen was the woman she wanted to spend the rest of her life with. Everything they'd gone through together had proved their bond ten times over.

Amber gazed down at her adoringly. She was still talking to her sister, no doubt reminding Jo to look after herself now that she was on her own and preparing to go off to college. The fact that Carmen was recuperating from a life-threatening injury hadn't stopped her from going out of her way to make sure that her sister was safe and happy.

Her self-sacrificing nature was a part of her that would never change. But what had changed was that she now had Amber to force her to put herself first now and then, to be there for her whenever she decided to jump in front of any bullets, real or metaphorical.

And given that Carmen was set on returning to her job as a bodyguard as soon as she was healed, there was a chance of that happening. But Amber had made her promise to only take safe contracts. She wouldn't be guarding Amber or anyone too high-profile anymore, but she'd still get to protect people. Amber couldn't stop her from doing that, even if she wanted to. It was who Carmen was. And her headstrong nature was the reason Amber had fallen in love with her in the first place.

Finally, Carmen gave her sister a farewell embrace, then watched her leave before returning to the house.

Amber smiled. Now, she had Carmen alone.

She headed to her wing, finding Carmen in their bedroom. Her back was turned, so she hadn't noticed Amber yet. She'd changed into a sports bra, which showed off her lean muscled back, and those tight black exercise pants. It was an outfit Amber hadn't seen her wearing in a long time. Carmen's doctor had instructed her to take it easy while she recuperated, which meant she was forbidden from exercising.

And Amber had kept a close eye on her to make sure she followed her doctor's instructions. She knew Carmen well enough. And Carmen liked to push herself. So Amber had spent the last couple of months making sure she didn't push herself harder than she could handle.

It was an uphill battle, given how stubborn Carmen was. And while she didn't always listen to Amber, she always listened to her Mistress.

Amber stepped into the room, her hands on her hips. "Where do you think you're going, dressed like that?"

Carmen jumped. "You scared me. My sister says hi, by the way."

Amber looked Carmen up and down. "Well?"

"I thought I'd get a workout in. And before you say anything, I've been cleared by the doctor for light exercise, starting today."

Amber shook her head. "Absolutely not. I know you. You don't know the meaning of light exercise. You're going to overdo it."

Carmen let out an exasperated sigh. "You're being ridiculous. If you had your way, I'd never be allowed out of bed."

"I'm trying to keep you from hurting yourself."

"And I appreciate the concern, but I assure you, I'm fine. I'm basically healed." Carmen swung her shoulder around. "See? I feel great."

Amber pursed her lips in thought. Perhaps she was being unreasonable. After all, her doctor had cleared her for exercise.

And exercise wasn't the only activity Carmen had been holding back on since her injury. Their intimate moments together had been somewhat restrained, and not in a good way.

But now that Carmen was healed...

"If you insist on getting a workout in, how about a workout of a different kind?"

Carmen tilted her head. "What do you mean?"

Amber took the strap of Carmen's sports bra, drawing it down her shoulder just an inch. "The kind of workout that allows me to make sure you can't push yourself too hard."

Carmen glanced around them, probably out of habit, then smiled. "What did you have in mind, Mistress Amber?"

"Playroom. Five minutes. Don't be late."

Exactly five minutes later, Carmen stood in the playroom, watching, entranced, as Amber unwound a coil of rope. It had been so long since she'd last set foot in this room, but it still provoked the same reaction in her, that same all-consuming desire she'd felt the first time she walked through the door with Amber.

"This is to make sure you can't move around too much," Amber said. "I wouldn't want you to hurt yourself." She set the rope on the bed, her eyes skimming up Carmen's body. "But first..."

Beckoning Carmen closer, she reached around to the back of Carmen's head, pulling her hair from its ponytail, letting it fall free over her shoulders. Then she took the bottom of Carmen's sports bra, pulling it up and over her head and tossing it aside. Goosebumps sprouted on her chest, exposed to the cool mansion air.

Amber picked the rope up from the bed, holding the long coil with both hands. "Turn around."

Carmen obeyed.

"And without the slightest hesitation," Amber said. "Usually, it takes much too long for me to unravel all those defenses of yours, to turn you into my pliant, obedient pet." She traced the backs of her fingers down the nape of Carmen's neck. "Does this mean you've finally learned to embrace your submissive side?"

Heat trickled down Carmen's back. Already, she felt the ache of anticipation, the intense craving for her Mistress's dominance. She had missed this. While her injury hadn't completely stopped the two of them from being intimate, it had forced them to be careful, gentle. But here, in this room, there was no holding back.

Amber took Carmen's arms and folded them behind her back, one on top of the other, and bound her wrists together. Then she took the rope and wound it around Carmen's chest, over and under her breasts and shoulders several times, securing her arms to her body.

"There." She turned Carmen around to face her. "That will keep you from overdoing it. Or from doing anything at all."

Amber brushed her hand over the ropes adorning her chest. As she reached Carmen's shoulder, her fingers drifted across to the scar there. Carmen shivered at her touch, light as a feather.

Amber pulled her hand back, concern written in her eyes. "Did I hurt you?"

Carmen shook her head. "Please don't stop. I need you so badly, Mistress."

Lust flashed in Amber's eyes. She pulled Carmen to the bed, pushing her backward onto it. Carmen drew in a gasp. With her arms restrained, she couldn't stop herself from falling.

But Amber didn't give her a chance to catch her breath. Slipping her knee between Carmen's thighs, she leaned down over her, her face inches from Carmen's, her gaze hungry.

Carmen rose to meet her, their lips colliding in an explosion of desire. Deep in her core, a fire flickered and flared. Amber's fingers twined in Carmen's hair as she devoured her lips, her tongue, her mouth. Her thigh pressed between Carmen's legs, stoking the flame pulsing there.

Carmen murmured drunkenly, arching into her, desperate to feel Amber's body against hers. Bound as she was, she could barely move, but that didn't stop her from trying.

Amber drew back until she was just out of Carmen's reach. "Looks like you're forgetting your place. We can't have that." She slid her hand down the center of Carmen's stomach, down to the peak of her thighs, stroking her through her leggings. "I've spent the last two months at your beck and call, waiting on you hand and foot. And while, as your girlfriend, I've enjoyed the chance to look after you for a change, as your Mistress, I can't have you forgetting which of us is in charge."

Carmen quivered, need swelling inside her.

But Amber just got up from the bed. "Besides, I'm not done making sure you can't hurt yourself further."

She crouched down and pulled a trunk out from underneath the bed. Inside was a collection of restraints—cuffs and shackles, straps and harnesses. Amber pushed them all aside and reached into the bottom of the trunk, withdrawing a long metal bar with a leather cuff attached at either end. A spreader bar.

She tossed it onto the bed beside Carmen's head. Carmen stared at it, her mouth gaping open. Her upper body was already completely immobilized. Amber wanted to restrain her legs too?

Amber folded her arms across her chest. "If you have something to say to your Mistress, now is the time."

Carmen's pulse skipped. The hard edge in Amber's voice was as much a warning as it was a challenge. She was pushing the limits of Carmen's comfort, and she knew it.

But Carmen wanted to be pushed. She wanted to be forced beyond those strict limits she imposed on herself, to be forced to let go and fall into her Mistress's control. Her need to always be on the defensive was something she would never completely shake. But with Amber, she could let her guard down. With Amber, she'd experienced the heights of pleasure and the depths of fear. Amber trusted her with her everything, even her life. And Carmen trusted her, too.

Amber gave her a firm look. "Well? Do you have anything to say?"

"No, Mistress," Carmen replied. "Please, keep going."

Satisfied, Amber reached down and stripped Carmen's leggings from her legs, taking her panties off with them. Then, she drew Carmen to the edge of the bed, leaving her legs hanging off the side of it, her feet flat on the floor.

Pulling Carmen's feet out wide, Amber took the spreader bar and secured the cuffs around each of Carmen's ankles. "There. Now I'm assured that you can't move around too much." She ran her hand down the front of Carmen's chest, trailing her fingertips over the ropes criss-crossing her skin. "And I'm going to make the most of having you at my mercy."

Heat rose from down in Carmen's center. Amber snaked her hand down between Carmen's breasts, down her stomach, past her belly button.

But at the very last moment, she pulled away.

Carmen groaned. Why did Amber feel the need to toy with her constantly? It was so infuriating.

It was so delicious.

"Believe me," Amber said. "You won't be complaining in a minute."

She took a step back and reached around behind her to unzip her dress. Slowly, sensually, she drew it up over her head and dropped it to the floor beside her. Her bra and panties followed, leaving her in nothing but her heels.

Carmen's lips parted in silent admiration. Amber's unashamed confidence, the way she wore her bare skin like a gown of fine silk, was mesmerizing.

Amber stepped between her legs and ran her hands down Carmen's thighs, pushing them apart even further.

Then, ice-blue eyes locked on Carmen's, she got down on her knees.

Carmen's pulse raced. Was Amber really doing this?

"Consider yourself lucky. It isn't often anyone gets to see me on my knees." She slid her hand up Carmen's inner thigh, her fingertips tickling her skin. "But how could I resist a taste of something so sweet, so forbidden?"

She leaned in and dipped her head between Carmen's legs, her warm lips grazing Carmen's folds. With painstaking slowness, Amber slipped her tongue into Carmen's slit, drawing it up and down in long, firm strokes, before gliding it up to tease her clit.

A moan spilled from Carmen's chest. She was so inflamed with lust that the pleasure of Amber's touch was almost unbearable. She clenched her legs reflexively, but the spreader bar at her ankles held them apart.

She whimpered. That only encouraged Amber. She wrapped her arms around Carmen's thighs, holding them apart even further, ravaging her with wild abandon. Carmen's legs trembled. She was speeding toward that blissful oblivion faster than she could handle.

But just as she approached it, Amber pulled back.

"I can't feel you this way," she said. "I need to feel you."

Rising to her feet, she leaned down over her, bracing her hands on the bed at either side of Carmen's head. Dipping down low, she pressed her lips to Carmen's, the scent and taste of her own arousal filling Carmen's head.

She rose into Amber, seeking her touch where she needed it the most. Without breaking the kiss, Amber snaked a hand down to where Carmen's thighs met, slipping her fingers inside her.

Carmen's mouth fell open in a soft sigh. With Amber inside her, the heel of her hand working her swollen clit, her soft lips consuming her, it was too much for her to take.

"Yes," she screamed. "Yes, Mistress!"

It only took seconds for her to come apart. Her body

stiffened, her toes and fingers curling as an orgasm overtook her. The cry that flew from her echoed through the room, the wing, the entire mansion. But she didn't care if anyone heard her. Nothing mattered in that moment, except the pleasure her Mistress was bestowing upon her.

Finally, Carmen crashed back down onto the bed. As Amber kissed her ravenously, a hunger came over her. Her earth-shattering climax had only made her desire for her Mistress more intense. She needed to give Amber what Amber had given to her, to bring her to the same heavenly heights, the same release that she'd brought Carmen to, not just now, but so many times before. And the urgency in Amber's kiss, her touch, told her that she hungered for that too.

Carmen murmured into her lips. "I want... I want to worship you."

Amber's chest hitched. She deepened the kiss, reaching around to Carmen's back, fingers scrabbling at the knots there in an attempt to free her.

But after a few seconds, Amber pulled away. "I don't have time for this." She reached for the nightstand and opened the top drawer, pulling out a pair of curved silver scissors. She brandished them before Carmen. "Don't move."

Carmen froze in place, heart pounding. Amber took the scissors and snipped through the ropes at her shoulders and the base of her sternum, the cold metal of the blades scraping along Carmen's skin. As the ropes fell away from her chest, Amber tore them from her body and arms, freeing her.

"I need you," she growled. "I need you right now."

Tossing the scissors aside, she grabbed Carmen's face in her hands, kissing her hard as she fell upon her. Their lips still locked, Amber drew her up the bed, falling back against the pillows and pulling Carmen onto her. Carmen's ankles were still locked in the spreader bar, her legs held open obscenely wide, but she barely noticed. All her attention was on the woman before her, the woman she belonged to. And she wanted to show Amber that she was her devoted servant.

She slid her hands up the front of Amber's body, from her knee, up her thigh, over her hips and waist, skating them up to her chest. She caressed Amber's breasts, tracing the pads of her fingers over each pale brown nipple, eliciting shivers from her. She mapped every stretch of her Mistress's skin with her fingertips, a reverent tenderness in her touch.

"Yes…" Amber's head rolled back. "Worship me, every part of me."

Carmen drew her lips down Amber's chin, down her neck, along her collarbone. She brushed her lips over Amber's breasts, painting kisses across her chest. She took a nipple in her mouth, rolling with her tongue, sucking with her lips.

Amber murmured blissfully, the sound reverberating into Carmen's body. She reached for Carmen, drawing her closer, holding her tighter. Her lips still playing at Amber's breasts, she ran her hands up to the peak of Amber's thighs, letting her fingertips skim the wetness between them.

Amber exhaled softly, parting her legs further, opening herself to her. Carmen slid her fingers up and down Amber's folds, rolling them over her clit, circling her entrance. But despite Amber's obvious desire, she didn't go any further, instead awaiting her Mistress's permission.

Amber reached down and took Carmen's chin, tipping her face up to look into her eyes.

"Fuck me," she commanded.

Carmen let out a trembling breath. Amber sat back, arms stretched out across the pillows at either side of her, as she waited for Carmen to obey.

Slowly, Carmen slipped her fingers into her. Amber pulsed around her fingers, warm, wet, welcoming. Carmen eased them in and out, tentatively at first, then more steadily. Amber rocked back against her, soft moans spilling from her, wordlessly directing Carmen's movements. *Faster,* she said. *Slower. Deeper.*

Carmen reveled in her Mistress's unbridled reactions. The arching of her back, the parting of her lips, the fevered cries falling from them. As Carmen brought her closer and closer to release, Amber wrapped her arms around her and pulled her into a fiery, aching kiss.

Finally, her arms wrapped tightly around Carmen's body, Amber went over the edge. Her hips rose from the bed as pleasure consumed her, sending tremors through her body that even Carmen could feel. Carmen worked her fingers inside her, drawing out her climax, until finally, it faded, and they collapsed into each other's arms.

Afterward, when they'd both recovered and Amber had freed her from her restraints, she pulled Carmen back down to the bed with her.

"Looks like your doctor is right," Amber said. "If you can do that, you're well and truly healed."

Carmen smiled. "It's all thanks to you. You've been

taking care of me all these weeks while I recovered. I can't begin to tell you how much I appreciate it."

"Considering you were injured saving my life, nursing you back to health was the least I could do. Besides, now that you're mine, taking care of you is my responsibility. And it makes me happy, because I love you."

"I love you too." Carmen would never tire of saying that. "And, I've kind of enjoyed having you take care of me. It isn't often that anyone does that." It wasn't often that she *let* anyone take care of her, or see her at her weakest. But she felt secure enough with Amber to let go around her.

Amber drew her into an embrace. "I'm glad you've enjoyed having me pamper you. And don't think this is going to end now that you're healed. Now that you belong to me, I'm going to spend every day spoiling you. So get used to it."

Carmen took a deep, satisfying breath and closed her eyes. "Yes, Mistress."

EPILOGUE

Gabrielle nudged Amber with her elbow. "When are you going to ask her?"

"Shh." Amber glanced around to make sure they hadn't been overheard. "I'm trying to keep things under wraps."

"You're not having second thoughts, are you?"

"No, I'm not. And given that we're at someone else's wedding, this is neither the time nor the place to discuss the matter."

Amber tipped her head toward Yvonne, who stood before a full-length mirror, clad in a white gown. It was her wedding day, and Amber was gathered with the other bridesmaids while they prepared for the ceremony. Madison, her maid of honor, was adjusting Yvonne's veil, while Lydia searched for extra hairpins.

Yvonne turned to face them. "What are you two whispering about?"

"Nothing," Amber said. "Don't mind us."

Yvonne raised a skeptical eyebrow. But she was quickly

distracted by Dana, who was scrutinizing the wedding dress she'd designed for her.

"Turn around," Dana said, brandishing a handful of pins. "I need to fix your dress."

Yvonne turned back to the mirror. Immediately, Gabrielle nudged Amber again.

"So what's the holdup?" she asked. "You've been carrying that ring around with you for weeks."

"I'm waiting for the right moment," Amber said. "That's all."

"Since when does Amber Pryce wait for anything? If you're stuck on proposal ideas, I have plenty of suggestions. We can come up with a grand proposal that Carmen will never forget."

"Carmen wouldn't want a grand proposal. And I don't need ideas."

"Are you afraid she'll say no?" Gabrielle asked. "Because the woman literally jumped in front of a bullet for you."

"That isn't quite what happened."

"It's close enough. My point is, what greater sign of dedication do you need?" Gabrielle paused. "Are you sure you're not having doubts?"

Amber shook her head. After all they'd been through together, she was certain of the strength of their relationship. She wanted, more than anything, to make Carmen hers.

So she'd set about doing just that, finding the perfect ring, getting Carmen's sister's approval. Even Amber's mother approved of the two of them tying the knot. For months, she'd been dropping not-so-subtle hints to Amber about asking Carmen to marry her. While the idea of settling down used to fill Amber with discomfort, now, spending the rest of her life with Carmen felt like the most natural thing.

So why was she hesitating?

Gabrielle gave her a sympathetic smile. "You know, it's okay to just be nervous. Committing to spending forever with someone is a big step to take."

"I am *not* nervous." Amber crossed her arms. "But you're right, this *is* a big step. It feels so monumental. So life-changing…"

As she fell silent, she realized that the room had gone quiet. All eyes were on her. Everyone had been listening to their conversation.

She sighed. *So much for keeping things under wraps.* "I didn't mean to distract everyone. Don't let me derail your preparations, Yvonne."

"It's all right," Yvonne said. "It's wonderful that you're thinking of proposing. And honestly, I could use a distraction from my nerves."

"You're nervous?" Amber asked. She didn't look it. The woman had nerves of steel.

"Of course I am," Yvonne replied. "You're right about one thing. The decision to get married is a monumental one. And it's not something that should be taken lightly, which is a lesson I learned all too well. But I also learned that you can't let fear stop you from embracing a life with the one you love."

Madison nodded. "And marriage *is* life-changing, in the best way possible. It will only make the love you share grow stronger. But no one can tell you if you're ready to take that step. Only you can."

"But I'm sure you already know the answer to that question," Lydia said. "Stop thinking and listen to your heart. What does it tell you?"

Amber closed her eyes for a moment, envisioning Carmen. "That I love her. That I want to be with her for the rest of our lives."

Gabrielle put her hand on Amber's arm. "And I'm sure Carmen feels the same way. When you look at her, and she looks at you, I can see it. And I know that the love between you is unbreakable. So listen to that love."

"You're right. Thank you, everyone." Amber's heart swelled. She was so fortunate to have friends like these. "Now, let's get back to preparations. We don't have long before the ceremony is due to begin."

"I'm all done with the dress," Dana said. "Yvonne, why don't you turn around and show everyone?"

Yvonne turned to face them, displaying her sleek, lace-covered gown. "How do I look?"

Lydia smiled. "Wonderful."

"Wow," Gabrielle said. "Just, wow."

Amber nodded in agreement. "You look beautiful."

Madison spread her arms out wide. "Look at you." She pulled Yvonne into an embrace, taking care not to disturb the dress. When Madison pulled away, her face was wet with tears. Would she be able to make it through the ceremony without crying her eyes out?

There was a knock on the door, followed by the voice of Blair, who was one of Ruby's bridesmaids. "Ruby is ready," she said. "If you're ready too, we can get started."

Yvonne nodded. "I'm ready."

Together, everyone left the room and headed outside.

They were on a small private island at the Greek Isles, the late afternoon sun hanging heavy in the sky. The wedding was taking place on a cliffside, overlooking the ocean.

After a brief delay, the ceremony began. Soon, Amber was standing by the altar with the other bridesmaids as the celebrant made his opening remarks. She couldn't help but feel moved by it, by this intimate celebration of love. It was a small wedding, just family and friends, but Yvonne had spared no expense in making it magical.

As the brides exchanged vows, Amber's gaze drifted out over the crowd, searching for Carmen. She found her sitting nearby, dressed in a pale blue dress, her wavy hair cascading freely over her bare shoulders, the warm sun streaming down onto her golden skin. The way her eyes glistened told Amber she was as moved by the proceedings as she was.

This side of Carmen, this softer side, was still something she rarely let anyone see, except for Amber. And it warmed her heart to know that Carmen felt comfortable enough in Amber's presence to show her that part of her. There were no boundaries, no walls between them any longer.

As if reading her mind, Carmen's eyes met hers. She smiled, a soft, radiant smile that stirred something deep in Amber's chest.

Listen to your heart. She couldn't deny what it was telling her right now.

Beside her, Ruby and Yvonne exchanged "I do's". The celebrant pronounced them married. And in front of an applauding crowd, they shared a passionate kiss.

And at that moment, Amber vowed that soon, it would be her at that altar with Carmen, saying *I do* and sealing their union with a kiss.

It was midnight when the reception finally ended. Carmen watched the brides depart, warmth spreading inside her. She'd never been the type to get emotional at weddings, but it was hard not to be affected by this celebration of love between two women she'd come to call friends. She'd spent enough time with Amber's friends now that she'd grown close with them, and she understood why Amber considered them family. She was starting to feel like they were her family, too. And seeing Yvonne and Ruby commit to each other for eternity was a beautiful thing.

She glanced at Amber beside her. The idea of committing to someone forever wasn't something Carmen had ever considered. She'd always had too many other priorities, too many responsibilities, to even allow herself to dream of such a thing.

But then, she'd met Amber. And 'forever' no longer seemed like a distant possibility.

Amber turned to her. "Shall we get out of here?"

Carmen nodded. "That bed in our suite is looking good right now."

"What's the hurry? It's such a nice night. Why don't we go for a walk down to the beach?"

Carmen studied her girlfriend's face. Amber wasn't the type to stop and enjoy the scenery. Perhaps Carmen wasn't the only one feeling sentimental tonight. "A walk on the beach sounds perfect."

They left the reception hall and made their way to the beach. Once they reached it, Carmen slipped out of her heels, holding them in her hand as she stepped onto the cool, white sand. Amber joined her, leading her down to where the ocean met the beach.

They walked along the sand in silence, gentle waves lapping at their feet, the half-moon shining above them. The beach was deserted. It was just the two of them.

Amber broke the silence. "Have I told you how wonderful you look tonight?"

"Only a dozen times," Carmen said. "I'm glad you appreciate it, because my feet are killing me. I don't know how you wear these heels all the time."

"Years of training, my love." Amber took her hand. "Aren't you supposed to be this strong, tough Marine? Surely you can handle wearing heels for a few hours."

"What can I say? My girlfriend has spoiled me so much that I've gone soft."

It had taken Carmen a long time to get used to being Amber's girlfriend and all the luxuries that entailed. Living in the mansion, attending fancy events, not as Amber's bodyguard, but as her partner. It had been an adjustment. But now, their life together felt comfortable and mundane in the most incredible way.

"Good," Amber said. "Because you deserve this. To enjoy life, to have all your needs taken care of, to not have to worry about a thing."

"You sound like my sister," Carmen said.

Jo had been away at college for a year now, and Carmen was still unused to it. Every time they spoke, her sister would remind her that now that she was gone, Carmen had no excuse for not living her life. It had taken months after her sister had left for her to stop feeling guilty about finally putting herself first. But Jo was living her own life now, and was doing fine, well even. So, for the first time, Carmen was free to focus on herself.

"Your sister is right. You don't need to sacrifice everything anymore, don't need to put anyone else first." Amber squeezed Carmen's hand. "You deserve happiness. You deserve the world."

"I don't want the world," Carmen said. "I only want one thing. And I have that right here."

Amber gave her a soft smile. They continued along the beach in comfortable silence. The stars were bright in the clear sky, and the sea breeze cooled the humid air.

Suddenly, Amber stopped in her tracks.

Carmen turned back to her. "Amber?"

But she just looked at Carmen, searching her face. There was something in her gaze, something wistful and longing, just like when they'd locked eyes during the wedding ceremony.

The moment stretched out in silence. Then, Amber released her hand and took a step back.

"I wasn't going to do this now," she said. "I was going to plan it all, so that everything was perfect..."

"Plan what?" Carmen asked.

Wordlessly, Amber dropped to one knee on the sand. Then, she produced a small box, opening it up and withdrawing a ring from it.

Carmen froze in place. *Is she... Is this...?*

Amber gazed up at her. "From the day I met you, I knew you were someone special. I was drawn to you, to your strength, your determination. But more than that, I was drawn to the vulnerability behind that strength, to the compassion and kindness that lies at the core of who you are. And I'm so honored that you trust me enough to share that part of yourself with me. I'm so honored that you're mine."

Carmen's heart began to pound. This was really happening.

"I love you more than words can express," Amber said. "I want you to be mine, and I want to be yours, not just right now, but for the rest of our lives. I want to wake up every morning with you by my side. I want to fall asleep every night with you next to me. I want to build a life with you, a family. I want to be with you, forever."

She reached out and took Carmen's hand. "Carmen Torres. Will you marry me?"

Carmen's heart surged. Suddenly, forming words seemed like the hardest thing. "Yes," she managed to whisper. "Yes. Yes, I'll marry you."

A warm smile grew on Amber's lips. She took the ring and slipped it onto Carmen's finger.

Rising to her feet, she swept Carmen into a deep, tender kiss that lingered on her lips long after it ended.

ABOUT THE AUTHOR

Anna Stone is the author of the bestselling Irresistibly Bound series. Her sizzling romance novels feature strong, complex, passionate women who love women. In every one of her books, you'll find off-the-charts heat and a guaranteed happily ever after.
Anna lives on the sunny east coast of Australia. When she isn't writing, she can usually be found with a coffee in one hand and a book in the other.

Visit annastoneauthor.com for information on her books and to sign up for her newsletter.

facebook.com/AnnaStoneRomance
twitter.com/AnnaStoneAuthor